We know every corner. We know the walls where you can hit a ball, all the good climbing trees, the short cuts and the long cuts, we know who makes good cookies. SHISH KABOB! I forgot. This is the title page!

45 + 47 Stella Street

and everything that happened

by

Henni Octon

(and Elizabeth Honey)

Annick Press Ltd.
Toronto • New York

We know where to ride our bikes to avoid the steep hills, where the milkweeds grow for Claire's canary. We know which drains will block in heavy rain, where Mr. Whippy stops, and the best places for roller blading. We know who gets drunk, which trees the cicadas will crawl up, and the best roof to watch the fireworks from.

J

Boy! Word sure travels fast around here!!!!!

Rob heard about my efforts so he bought meXKXX
this old tyXXpewriter at an auction.
$5!!! It's a loud clunky old heaXp. When
I hit the keys it's like guns going off.

The words still don't look like theyXX
do in a book but it sure beats the pen,
(and my writing!)

And Donna has volunteered to photocopy it
at work as long as she gets a copXy.

Everyone knows I want to be a writxer like
my hero Gillian Rubinstein. Well, here&s
my chance.

Contents I'll write them in as I go.

Goodbye Old Clatterbash! Hello to The Miracle!

Tibor heard about my efforts.
'Don't waste your time on that old dinosaur,' he said.
'If you're going to write our story you may as well do it so we can read it.'

He showed me how to work his Apple Mac which he said I can use any day after school. It is *pure magic!*
I can't believe what this thing can do!!!!!!!!!!!!!!!!!!!!!!!!!!
growl, *sing*, **be funny**, shout, whisper.
It's so instant and so easy!

This is going to be a zillion times better than I thought it would be.

Tibor showed me how to set it out so it looks professional, and when it's finished he says he knows someone who will bind it for me! It will be a REAL BOOK! Honestly, I am in Heaven.

Dear God,

Sometimes I wonder about this. Is Heaven really good? Because I don't see how it could be any better than this. I don't think I could be happier. You never hear about people working in Heaven. It sounds like total retirement. If it's all the same with you I'd much rather be doing something. Do they have computers in Heaven? I hope so.

Henni

1

Introductions

Hi I'm Henni I'm high I'm Henni
I'm high I'm Henni I'm high Hi

I'm the tallest girl in our school. I'm not the oldest or the cleverest or the prettiest or the funniest but I sure am the tallest which nobody can deny.

I don't mind being tall because my best friend is most unusual too when you first meet him. And I like being unusual together. Besides unusual people turn out to be usual when you get to know them.

Zev is my best friend. He is the most unusual person I've ever met.

He is the happiest boy with the sweetest nature which sounds really soppy but he is. His mother and father wanted to have a whole football team of children but there was only Zev, so he got enough love for a whole football team. That may have something to do with it.

Zev hates a fuss but there is something *amazing* about him. He has electric hair. It stands straight up. When he was a baby his mother noticed that when she combed it she got a little shock. Zev always looks as if he's just had a shock.

For example, we were at this person's place and there was something on the TV which we didn't want to watch and Zev combed his hair and there was such snow on the screen the man couldn't figure out what the hell was going on, and the lady says, 'Electricity in the air!' And Zev whispers, 'Electricity in the hair!'

If he combs his hair he can make any radio crackle like mad.

And at night, like for example when we were at camp, we turned off the light and all the kids yell, 'Comb your hair Zev! Go on! Comb your hair!'
And when he does, a brilliant spray of coloured sparks shoots out like a fireworks display.
Honest to God, I kid you not!

Once, Zev was at the movies and in the middle of a gunfight in a tornado the man sitting next to him collapsed. Just upped and flopped. Fortunately there was a doctor nearby who tried to help him. He yells out, 'He's had a heart attack and his heart has stopped! Quick! Call an ambulance!'

Well, Zev reads lots of books about electricity and when he's alone he conducts little experiments on his hair. Anyway at this movie where the bloke collapsed, Zev ripped a comb through his hair ten times and touched him. And with a sudden jerk the man popped up like a jack-in-a-box. 'Phew!' he said. 'What happened?'

'Your heart stopped,' said the doctor, 'and this lad here...he...'

But Zev was gone. Like I said, he hates a fuss. That's what I heard happened.

I wasn't there but the other kids swore it was all true.

I will tell you a secret that absolutely nobody knows...if you absolutely promise promise promise not to tell anyone.

Zev has this *fantastic* collection of combs.

Next-door to Zev lives Mr Nic. Real name: Mr Valentine Nicnac. Mrs Nic died of cancer years ago and there are no little Nics. But in many ways Mr Nic is like a kid. He gets so gleeful when things work out. He used to work at the railways but now he teaches piano.

Parents think he's wonderful because he gets the little kids hooked on piano. But just when the kids are getting pretty swinging in a loud sort of honky tonk, make-it-up-as-you-go-along way and really having fun the parents whip them over to a respectable piano teacher with clean fingernails, who sets lots of scales and says 'I think we should aim for the Grade 3 music exam next June.' But Mr Nic is a cheerful chap, and says 'Something will turn up' (which it always does).

And next door to Mr Nic is 47.

Kids love 47 Stella Street. It is like dreams come true. Frank lives at 47. He's six. His dad, Rob, is a junk dealer. Their house is a big old rambling, tumbled-down, fixed-up, crazy place. If a board falls off the wall Rob nails a sign over the hole. A window got broken once and he replaced it with a milk bar window. He fixes things in his own way.

Frank's mum, Donna, loves gardening. She plants something in every piece of junk that can hold even so much as an egg cup of soil.

Petunias bloom from the back of a merry-go-round swan, sweet peas climb up from a rocket. An old cart busts with pansies. Blooms tumble out of a set of cups and a broken teapot, a wheelbarrow, boots, an electric jug, espresso coffee machine, and onions sprout up from a rusty old pop-up toaster.

One corner of the backyard is her huge pile of dirt and the compost.

She has these old children's rides from the supermarket, a fire engine, Bambi, Dumbo, Giraffe, two little pigs and a donkey, and they all have little gardens in them.

Spring is wonderful at 47. All the junk bursts into bloom.

Once there was an article on Donna's garden in a magazine and the heading was 'A Blossoming Passion for Things Past'.

I've done all this babbling on and I still haven't started the story.

2

Goodbye Old Auntie Lillie

Once upon a time (this is true though) Rob knocked on Old Auntie Lillie's door and she didn't answer so he went inside and there she was lying on the kitchen floor with her hands clasped like Snow White's and her sweet half-smile on her face, except she wasn't waiting for a prince to kiss her, she was as dead as a door nail.

Old Auntie Lillie had lived in Stella Street for ages and ages. Centuries. She was *THE* original resident. (I've done my research.) There was an Uncle Les, but Uncle Les was lost during the war, and a good thing too, according to Mr Nic.

Old Auntie Lillie always bought school raffle tickets, and she sponsored us for school spell-a-thons, or read-a-thons, or lap-a-thons, or whatever thons we were having. (This is a write-a-thon!) And every Christmas she gave all the kids in Stella Street $2. And she was happy to look after our pets if we went on holidays.

Old Auntie Lillie always had a little smile on her face, like those madonnas in paintings by the great masters. They always wear those soft sweet half-smiles no matter what the little Baby Jesus is doing. And he spent a lot of time (if you believe the paintings) without a diaper on, so I reckon there would have been times when there was a lot going on behind that smile. I think there was with Auntie Lillie too.

So there was a big funeral for Old Auntie Lillie, with masses of flowers and *everybody* from Stella Street was there. 'It is sad,' they said, 'but that is the way to go. Suddenly. On your own kitchen floor (and it was clean too) smiling in your sleep.The dear old thing had lived a good life. She was getting on. Way to go,' etc, etc, etc, etc, etc. But it was so sad.

So her house was empty.

Dear God,

I hope you're given Old Auntie Lillie a good spot up there. She didn't do massive good works, but she was always kind to us kids. I never heard her say anything bad about anyone and she went to church every Sunday. But I guess you know all this.

Tell her we miss her.

We really do.

Over and out,

Henni

3

Old Auntie Lillie's place gets the treatment

We weren't there and we didn't see it but Old Auntie Lillie's place suddenly had the guts ripped out of it. At the front the house still had the same lovely old face but the back part, the little porch, the kitchen, the bathroom, the laundry—gone! The tiles, cupboards, sink, stove, the windows and the lino that Old Auntie Lillie kept so clean all those years were wrenched out in one day. Smashed and broken and heaved into the back of an AAAABABA Ezy Dump truck and taken to the dump. We saw the last truckload go when we arrived home from school.

We couldn't believe our eyes. Zev's hair stood up even more on end.

Auntie Lillie's looked like a tornado had clean ripped off the back. It was raw and wounded. We just stared at it feeling winded as if we'd come off the monkey bars flat onto the ground. And we felt even sadder about Old Auntie Lillie.

We went to Zev's and had banana smoothies with a big scoop of ice-cream for the bad news.

Who was going to live in 45?

'Maybe they have stacks of kids,' said Frank hopefully, 'and they're going to build this huge playroom at the back.'

'No,' said Zev. 'It's a mountain climber who fell off a mountain in a terrible accident and has to have ramps and bars and all the stuff you need when you get around in a wheelchair.'

'It's somebody with important pedigree dogs,' said Danielle, 'and they need special dog doors and dog baths and dog beds.'

We were all dead curious I can tell you.

One thing we *did* know was whoever it was had plenty of money.

Then the building started. First trucks and diggers, and a Port-a-Toilet in the front garden, then bricks, wire, boards, dirt, garbage, electrical wires going in and out of the house like spaghetti. For a couple of months 45 was a real mess. Once the walls went up we couldn't see what was going on inside. Hammering, sawing, drilling. NOISE! NOISE! NOISE! And the builders had their beaten up radio going all the time on a rock station mega mega LOUD! They had to have it loud so they could hear it above the racket they were making.

We still didn't know who was going to live there. Donna who's really friendly, and can talk to anyone, talked to the builders all the time but they didn't want to talk about the owner.

One afternoon Rob heard an argument in 45. A lot of shouting. A woman shrieked 'Is that the best you can do?' and a man yelled, 'You fix it or I fix you!'

Then vans began delivering all this new stuff to 45, like ants carting crumbs down their hole. Everything was absolutely brand new, in its box.

We made this fantastic fort for Frank out of the boxes, with doors between the rooms.

We made a game out of it.

Me: Hi Zev. How's your new stove?

Zev: Hi Henni! How's your new dishwasher?

Frank: Hi Henni and Zev. How's your new four-storey fridge?

Zev: Hi Henni. How's your new range hood?

Me: Hi Frank and Zev. Wrong fridge! Got another new four-storey fridge!

Zev: Hi Henni! How's your new freezer?

Then this day Zev comes racing up .

Hi Henni! How's your NEW SATELLITE DISH!!!!!!!!!!!!!!!
!!

Me: WOW!

Zev: WOW AND WHY?

Boy did that get us wondering! What were they going to do in there?

Watch sports all day? R-rated movies? Stella Street with a satellite dish! That was news!

Stay tuned. Beam in. You ain't heard nothin' yet.

Zev started getting books out of the library about satellites.

4

New neighbours

We smelt her first. Danielle, Zev, Frank, Briquette (Frank's dog) and I were walking down the back lane to Zev's place when the new roller garage door at 45 starts gently gliding up and we get a noseful of this smell like a pharmacist's where someone's tried on *all* the sample perfumes. The door glides up higher and we see this pair of gold shoes, and bit by bit we see this person revealed. We looked at her and she looked at us. She had fluffed-up hair like blonde candy floss. You could sort of see through it. And her eyebrows were very black and her mouth was very red and her earrings and necklaces were very very gold and her nose was like a 2H pencil.

Briquette gave a low growl.

Danielle said 'Hello.' And Mrs New Next-door said 'Hello' and looked at Briquette, then she got into her new silver car. And we walked on to Zev's place.

'What do you think?' I asked.

'Well she wears too much perfume,' said Zev.

'She stinks,' said Frank.

'She wears too much perfume because she farts a lot,' said Danielle. That's Danielle for you.

'Be fair,' I said (I'm a very fair person—I think it's part of being tall), 'I think she looked pretty harmless. Don't judge a book by its smell.'

'Dogs do!' said Frank.

Then the New Next-doors had the house painted totally white. Totally completely blanco, inside and out. Like a science laboratory, so anything, even the tiniest little dust mite would show up.

Then they had the garden dug up by a landscape gardening man and a path made from the gate to the front door with a tree on either side. Zev heard what happened when the landscape gardener thought he had finished the garden and Mrs New Next-door starts raving about how one of the trees on one side of the path wasn't the same shape as the tree on the other side of the path. We checked it out and it looked OK to us.

But Mrs New Next-door bawled out the landscape man and he went away and came back with two new trees and dug up the others and planted the new ones in their place, and quite frankly I couldn't see the difference. Actually it looked quite nice, rather neat and lovely like something from the cover of a magazine.

About this time Zev and I were going to the library and we walked past Mr New Next-door. He said 'Hello children' in a no-nonsense voice. He was quite handsome in a dark stoneface kind of way. He wasn't tall. His eyes and his eyebrows and his mouth were all parallel like cowboys and men in whisky ads.

Then the New Next-doors had the new front fence built. It was brick with iron bars, like spears, in between big brick posts. The big brick gate posts had a place on top obviously left for some decoration.

Here's what we guessed:

Rob - lions

Zev - eagle with serpents

Frank - big concrete bottles of perfume

Danielle - love hearts

Donna - cupids and urns with gorgeous trailing roses

Briquette - bones

Here's what they did put:

Big balls!

They looked *wrong*.
They were *much* too big for the posts.
They looked *stupid*.

Then the painters arrived in a paint-speckled van. One of the painters was a lady with big bouncing breasts and she was wearing this tee-shirt with Nepal on it and these mountains were bouncing all around. The fence, the gate and the balls were all painted white. Then Mr New Next-door came steaming out and said it wasn't white enough, and bouncing mountains told him where to get off, and the painters jumped in their speckled van and drove off with a screech. But next morning the man painter was back and he put on another whole coat of white paint.

Then they had the white carpet put in which was pretty radical. Up came a big furniture van and out came all Old Auntie Lillie's carpet with the flowers on it, and in went these big rolls of perfectly white carpet. It must have been as if a new carpet of snow had fallen all through their house. (Like that bit of poetic writing?) From then on they probably didn't eat beetroot or tomato or spaghetti or any of those dangerous foods. They probably lived on white food like boiled rice and vanilla ice-cream just to be on the safe side.

Old Auntie Lillie's place
45
Before
45
After

5

The Phonies

So there are the New Next-doors in this fantastic swanky villa that used to be Old Auntie Lillie's house. Now they have their friends around for tea, sorry *dinnah*, so they can show off how fantastic their new house is. They are so *nace* and 'Hello *Daaaaarling*' and 'Wonderful to *seeeeeeeeeee* you' and *Daaaarling* this and *Daaaarling* that and *Daaaarling* everything else and all that fluffy talk.

You're probably thinking what a snoopy little pack of eavesdroppers we are. We're not. (Well, we weren't then!) We just couldn't help overhearing.

Me and Danielle and Zev were babysitting Frank because Donna had had a hard week, when the New Next-doors have some wonderful, very very dear close sweet lovely friends around for dinnah. We're splitting our skins watching 'The Gods Must Be Crazy' on TV. Frank's asleep on the couch and it's getting a bit late. We hear all the very very dear close friends climb into their fossil fuellers and Range Rovers (which have never roved a range in their lives!) and doors slam, slam, slam and 'Bye bye Daaaalings,' 'Bye bye Shareena,' 'Bye bye,' etc, etc, etc, etc.

THEN we hear the New Next-doors go inside. Suddenly the air turns red and they're having this MIGHTY SCREAMING MATCH!

'*NEVER* again!' '*WHO* invited *THEM*!' 'Whose *STUPID* idea was it in the first place?, etc, etc, etc. Some of the descriptions of the daaarling guests were so good we started writing them down.

Your &****$#@$%* idiot work scumbags!

Those mean pig-nosed snivelling **&✠★#& slobs!

That pansy, pasty, two-faced (TWO-FACED! Pretty good coming from them!)****#@✠▼&$*% fawning insect!

#***✠❞▲$&*# overbearing spiteful, lily-livered jellyfish weasel! (Jellyfish are beautiful creatures.)

That foul-mouthed (now who's calling the pot black!) *%$#@✠✂❞$&#*** rancid old bat

Rotting, contaminated ***❄❄✠%&#* skeleton!

✱❄✱&&* pimply incompetent *@✠*✱✂ technological dreg

Sleazy, shifty, ferret-nosed **&%✠@#* greasy ape!

Spineless, chinless, gutless, legless *$✠@#** octopus!

Pretty good aren't they!

I can't write all they really said in case innocent little children chance to pick up this book, but you get the picture. Outside everything's Daarling. Inside everything's Scumbag. Wow! We were knocked out! That's when we started calling them the Phonies.

Ron and Donna came home all happy and funny and silly and we told them about how we'd watched 'The Gods Must be Crazy' and then listened to 'The Neighbours Must be Crazy' and we all had a good laugh.

(Six 'ands' in one sentence! I'll never get to be Gillian Rubinstein!)

All was quiet on the Phonie front for a week then something happened that made Mrs Phonie hopping mad. She threw out a saucepan, and presto, next day she saw it in Donna's garden with a zinnia sticking out of it.

Instantly she marches in.

'What do you mean by planting things in my garbage?'

'You threw it out,' said Donna in a reasonable way. 'I could have got it from the dump but I took it from the front lawn. I think it looks rather good.'

'It looks ri*di*culous! Absolutely ri*di*culous!' she snapped. 'Please do not interfere with our garbage again,' and she storms off.

The Phonies had so much garbage! Stuff that wasn't even used. Perfectly good stuff. They didn't give it to the Salvation Army or the Red Cross or the thrift shop, they just put it in the garbage can!

Dear God,
When the Phonies get to Heaven have St Peter meet them at the ~~Pur~~ Pearly Gates and say 'Is this your garbage?' And have all their garbage piled up there. I warn you God it's going to be a pile a thousand metres high. And ask St Peter to ask them if they cared about the planet and ask St Peter to ask them if they cared about other people.
Signing out, Henni

So, as you can see, they weren't the neighbours we had in mind.

6

The side fence

The fence between 45 Stella Street and 47 Stella Street had a lean to it, but it was a fair lean. It leaned towards the Phonies for half its length, and towards Rob and Donna for the rest of its length.

This day Zev and Frank stomp into our kitchen and flop down. They look as happy as a bag of old mushrooms. Bad news. So we make ourselves chocolate milk and put in an extra spoonful to calm the nerves.

Rob, Frank's dad, had a bad day. First he bought an old chest of drawers at an auction, then found out it had borer (which is little worms that eat through the wood and make little holes in it) so it wasn't worth nearly as much as he paid for it, then he drove to Palaver Hills, which is in the Outer Galaxies, to deliver some chairs but the guy wasn't home and there was nowhere safe where he could leave them so it was a wasted trip, then, when he jumped back into his truck he sat on his sandwiches.

So he comes home tired and dejected, and Donna, who's been flat out playing Happy Families at work, didn't get to the shops so it's tinned soup for supper.

Then Rob opens up the mail.

The first letter is council rates which have gone up.

The second letter is a phone bill which is big because Donna organised Old Auntie Lillie's funeral.

The third letter...PTO

HOOK, RUTHERFORD & SMEETON

BARRISTERS & SOLICITORS

550 Collins Street
Melbourne, Victoria 3000
Telephone: (03) 629 5061
Facsimile: (03) 614 9365

The owner,
47 Stella Street,
Baker's Hill, Vic.

Our Ref:RS:941028
15 May

Dear Sir / Madam,

RE: 45 - 47 STELLA STREET, PARTY FENCE REPLACEMENT

My client instructs me to inform you that the above-mentioned fence is dangerous, an eyesore, in total disrepair and in urgent need of replacement.

My client requests that I inform you that, pursuant to that end, we have obtained a quote from a reputable local fencing contractor. The total cost, including preparation, labour, materials, and painting thereof, is $4890, this sum to be divided equally between the two parties in respect of this affair.

Trusting this meets with your approval,

RSmeeton

ROBERT SMEETON

BH:kh

'No it doesn't meet with my approval,' says Rob sort of sadly.

'What does it mean?' asks Frank.

Donna explains. 'The Phonies want a new side fence built. It will cost $4890. They expect us to pay half.' She turned to Rob. 'Nearly five thousand bucks for a new fence is a bit steep isn't it?'

'Steep!' says Rob. 'It's VERTICAL!'

Rob says, 'And why didn't they just say "Let's talk about a new fence!" instead of coming out guns blazing with all this solicitor's letter nonsense.'

'They're probably shy,' says Donna unconvincingly.

'Yeah,' says Rob who goes off muttering 'Nearly five thousand bucks! They must be made of money! What are they going to build it out of? Solid gold?'

Calling Golf Oscar Delta...
Calling Golf Oscar Delta.

We've got a problem here.

A. Rob doesn't want a new fence. He likes the old one. He says it will stand for another 50 years.

B. Anyway he hasn't got the money to pay for a new one.

C. $4890 is a mighty lot of money for a new fence.

Got any suggestions?

Over and out,
Hotel Echo November November Igloo

7

Briquette's banquet

I keep wanting to tell the story but then I remember that I haven't told who people are. In books they do that so smoothly you never have to stop and say who on earth is that? Well, I'm not that good yet.

Mum and Dad. They haven't come into the story yet. But I'm not an orphan.

Danielle. She's my little sister. She's nine. She's a bit of a pain and she gets away with a lot. She has a shrill scream like an umpire's whistle. She is bold and sometimes she's really rude. But she's funny too. She says what she thinks and sometimes that's what everybody thinks, but she's the only one that will say it aloud.

And another thing about my nutcase sister (I could write 500 pages about her) she loves music. She's bananas about this wild group that nobody knows about called Noyzeeboys. They have this hit 'Check out the Exit'. I like it too but she's crazy about it. She jumps to the radio and turns it up whenever it comes on and dances around like an electrified rag doll. She's a fantastic neat dancer. But in ordinary life she is really unco-ordinated. Always dropping things.

Donna's work. Donna works at this social service sort of office which is where they try and solve terrible human problems. Sort of like playing Happy Families only with real families and she tries to patch them up and put them together again. Sometimes Rob and Donna have kids staying with them while things at her work get sorted out. Sometimes some of these kids are a bit off the planet. But Donna just gets them out in her garden planting stuff and watering and yakking away.

We call them rent-a-kid.

Zev and Frank spend a lot of time together because Frank goes to Zev's place after school because Donna works.

Briquette. She's Rob and Donna and Frank's black sausage dog. But she's everybody's dog. We all look after her. She goes visiting, especially Mr Nic. We look after her when Rob and Donna and Frank go camping where you can't take dogs. Briquette is shiny, black and gallops around the place with her funny little sausage dog gallop, black ears and pink tongue flapping and this loopy grin on her face. She thinks life is FANtastic! And she is a greedy little pig. A long stomach on short legs. Gulp gulp gulp goes Briquette, and shazzam the bowl is empty, and she looks up at you with that lopsided grin saying 'MORE?'

'Wish I enjoyed my food so much,' says Mr Nic who has a tender tummy and is always slotting in a Mylanta tablet. That's probably why he feeds her junk. He watches her enjoy all the things he can't have.

Danielle reckons Briquette's motto is 'Yum yum yum'.

'It's "Live to eat!",' says Zev.

Then Frank starts singing 'Eat it' to that Michael Jackson song.

Everyone on Stella Street has stories of the disgusting things Briquette has eaten (or rolled in). She trots around so pleased with herself. She's supposed to stay in but she gets out. She only goes to visit her friends and she never annoys anyone or crosses the road.

Meanwhile back at the story—I said that the Phonies threw out tons of stuff. Well they also threw out *heaps* of food. We reckoned they should take their garbage cans to the supermarket and stick them in the cart and heave the food straight in. That would save them the bother of opening it.

They chucked out stuff that was hardly touched. It was disgusting!

Talking of disgusting...

If disgusting dog behaviour upsets you - **SWITCH OFF NOW!!**

So, cool detective dudes, you have probably realised that it's a deadly combination we have here. Dynamite and the match! The Phonies' garbage and Briquette!

This particular day Danielle and I are trudging home from school when we turn the corner and what do we see in front of the Phonies? Nightmare on Stella Street!

Garbage spread all over the footpath and both the Phonies' cans are down and in the middle of the mess is Briquette. She's pigging out on the Sara Lee cheese cake, gulp gulp gulp, Chicken Tonight this afternooon, gulp gulp gulp, bacon rinds, stinking runny cheese, Cocktail Satay Delights, gulp gulp gulp, and her tail's straight out and she's going like mad because she knows it can't last and we're yelling '*GET OUT OF IT BRIQUETTE!*'

Danielle scrambles in to grab her and knocks a can which rolls into the gutter spewing more garbage everywhere, and Briquette's into the meat balls stroganoff, gulp gulp gulp, more cheese cake, gulp gulp gulp, and she's slippery as a fish. I try and grab her, slip on a quiche, land on a lettuce and then THE PHONIES DRIVE UP! They stand there so shocked at this godawful mess that is their garbage and this black sausage dog who's swelled up like a black balloon who's still going for it, gulp gulp gulp...

Mrs Phonie screams, 'GET THAT DOG AWAY! I've had a GUTFUL!'

She wasn't the only one.

Briquette stops, looks up at her, then with one convulsive heave chucks up everything she's eaten at Mrs Phonie's feet. And gulp gulp gulp *STARTS TO EAT IT AGAIN!!!!!!!!!!!!*

Mrs Phonie screams as if she's being murdered. We nearly died. (We nearly did die laughing later on.) People come running.

Mr Phonie says in a deathly whisper, 'You've got fifteen minutes to fix this,' then grabs Mrs Phonie and wheels her inside.

We scramble around, frantic. Mr Nic grabs the hose at Rob and Donna's. Danielle chucks Briquette in Rob's shed and we're sweeping and scooping. Mum grabs some new garbage bags and we shove it all in them. Zev and Frank run up and we're all cleaning in a frenzy. It's back in the cans and twelve minutes later it's all over.

The front lawn is wet and the gutter hosed down.

Nobody would know it had happened *except*, the picture of Briquette pigging out, then chucking it up and Mrs Phonie's face, is etched on our memory for ever and ever.

That afternoon was also indelibly etched onto another memory too. Briquette's. She's had the banquet of her life. She's hooked. She now lives for the Phonies' garbage. She longs for it. She dreams of it. In her basket at night she sleepeats. Her little legs twitch and run, she drools, and her choppers gobble.

When Rob and Donna get home they are MORTIFIED when they hear what happened. Straight away they go and knock on the Phonies' door and apologise, and Frank, the little knucklehead, thinking that it might soften them up a bit says

'Briquette is sick.'

'The little pig deserves to die,' says Mrs Phonie.

'Painfully,' says Mr Phonie, and slams the door.

8

A lick and a wish

For a while after Briquette's banquet everyone in Stella Street tried to be super-friendly to the Phonies, but we didn't get a chance. They ignored us. It was like smiling at a brick wall. Anyway, they were hardly ever there. Besides, deep deep down, at this point, I think we decided, for real, we didn't like them.

Briquette's banquet *was* a rough scene for the Phonies, but it was cleaned up lightning fast. If it wasn't for their stupid garbage it wouldn't have happened anyway. Everyone who has dogs or cats knows that it's not all roses.

'When they were kids were their pets perfect?' said Frank.

'I bet they were revolting,' I said.

'They wouldn't have had pets,' said Zev.

'I bet they weren't even kids,' said Danielle. 'They came straight from the Evil Planet.'

Besides we reckoned the Phonies owed Rob and Donna a few favours. When the builders were working on Old Auntie Lillie's place Rob helped when they needed an extra pair of hands ***AND*** their trucks were always blocking Rob and Donna's drive ***AND*** the builders always arrived very early in the morning and woke them up ***AND*** they left messages with Rob and Donna ***AND*** they knocked a branch off Rob and Donna's apricot tree ***AND*** did Rob and Donna complain?

NOT ONCE!

But nobody mentioned that.

Rob went round the fence at 47 blocking up all the places where Briquette gets out, so Briquette scratches at the gate, whimpering and barking. She runs back and forwards, back and forwards, back and forwards along the front fence, barking, barking, barking.

Look at it from Briquette's point of view. One day everyone's her friend and life's free and easy then ***SHAZZAM!***— she's locked up all by herself.

The people she used to visit miss her but either they don't know what happened or they can't be bothered coming to see her, except for Mr Nic who babysits Briquette. He leads her home to his place and carefully locks the gate.

If she gets out she's gallopy-gallop back to the Phonies. She thinks that dream day just might happen again, and when it does, she's going to be there. She jumps up and down at the Phonies' front gate barking her head off.

'Aff aff! Yoohoo! ***Aff aff aff!*** It's me again! ***Aff aff aff!*** Roll out the garbage. ***Aff aff!*** I'm starving! ***Aff aff aff!'***

THEN Rob and Donna get another letter, this time from the Council.

'Those bloody ratbags,' says Rob. 'It's getting to the stage where I don't want to open the mail any more. It's all bad news.'

Donna is silent. She's thinking she has enough trouble at work dealing with screwballs who don't know how to get along with others and now she's getting it on the home front too.

CITY OF BARRIMA

Town Hall, High Street, Baker's Hill 3771
Ausdoc DF98459
Facsimile: 731 9922

Your Ref:

Our Ref: 60/001/004/001

Refer:

24 June

Donna and Robert O'Sullivan
47 Stella Street
Baker's Hill Vic 3771

Dear Ms. and Mr. O'Sullivan:

The Office of Environmental Health Department has received serious complaints about your dog. The complaints include excessive barking, creating a serious public nuisance, interfering with residents' garbage, and wandering at large in the neighbourhood.

If found guilty of an offence the owner is liable to prosecution.

THE FOLLOWING NOTE ON THE DOG ACT OFFENCES ARE GIVEN FOR YOUR INFORMATION;

DOG ACT OFFENCES

ON THE SPOT NOTICES CAN BE ISSUED FOR ANY OF THE FOLLOWING OFFENCES :

Section of Dog Act	Nature of Infringement	Penalty
11	Owner's name and address not on registration collar	$50
12	Registered dog outside owner's premises without registration collar	
13	Unregistered dog wearing registered collar	
14	Person defacing registration badge	
16 (1) (a)	Dog on premised of a School or Shop	
16 (1) (b)	Dog in or about Railway Station or in Shopping area not on leash	
15	Dog at large outside owner's premises during daytime	$100
19	Greyhound outside owner's premises not muzzled or under effective control	
4	Failure to register dog	$200
15	Dog at large outside owner's premises at night time	

I wish to inform you that, unless effective control is exerted immediately, further action will be taken.

Yours faithfully

W. Burgess

W.P. Burgess
Environmental Health Department

'What are they going to complain about next?' says Rob. 'Tomorrow there'll be a letter saying "There are people next door breathing and we just can't stand it. Send in the Terminator".'

'Could they fine us a large amount of money?' asks Donna. 'Could they take Briquette away? What are we going to do?'

'What are we going to do?' says Rob. 'We could give Briquette away, we could move, we could have her put down, but I'll tell you what we're going to do,' says Rob. 'Nothing.'

* * *

Danielle and I were cleaning up my room. This happens about every couple of centuries, usually when a library book gets mixed up with our books and the library fine has got to $250,000 and we just *have* to find that book.

Or something else goes seriously missing like my watch, or $10. So we dump everything out of the drawers and off the shelves and the room looks like a bomb hit it, and we sort through it all and find all these favourite old toys and games and stuff we haven't seen for ages and ages. A lot of Danielle's stuff is in my room too because her room is smaller. I've got the big bookcase in my room.

'Oh, my little old giraffe I used to take to bed with me every night when I was four,' squeals Danielle.

'My fruit earrings I got in the party fish pond!' I cry. (This is old book talk: she cried, they cried. I'm sick of saying said and says all the time. I'm desperate to find another word. Wonder if Gillian Rubinstein has the same problem with said and says?)

'My dead moth collection!' (except some of them weren't dead and they'd eaten holes in Danielle's knitted Minnie Mouse.)

'The dinky hankies!' (You know those pretty hankies you get given with little flowers and lace on them, but one blow and the snot shoots right through them. Hopeless. Nobody ever uses them.)

'My hula Barbie!' etc, etc, etc, etc.

Frank and Zev and Briquette come in, scrape a hole in the junk and plonk down. Frank immediately starts playing with Danielle's Polly Pockets and Briquette is sniffing round for bits of hundred-year-old Easter egg, but Zev is here on business.

'What are we going to do about Briquette and the Phonies?' says Zev.

'I've been trying my best to forget the Phonies,' I cry. 'It's not fair! People can complain about dogs but dogs can't complain about people!'

'They can bite them,' said Danielle.

'That's sure death,' said Zev.

(Those fearful words reminded us of something we'd all thought, but nobody had said.) Briquette's still snuffling.

'We could make this petition saying I HATE THE STINKING PHONIES and get everybody to sign it,' says Danielle.

'Then what would you do with it?' I ask.

'Send it to Parliament.'

'Oh yeah, great stuff. Ladies and Gentlemen of the Government of Australia, I have here a petition signed by seven zillion loyal citizens who hate the Phonies.'

'We could write to that lady in the Women's Weekly who tells you what to do about problems,' I suggest.

'Yeah, but that's about babies and boyfriends and sex,' says Danielle.

Then Zev has this stroke of brilliance.

'We could write to the Ombudsman.'

'The who?'

'The Ombudsman. He's sort of like an umpire of justice. I heard about him at school. He doesn't know either side of the fight and he hears the story and tells you what he thinks is a fair thing. And he's free. You don't have to pay him.'

'You don't have to pay to write to people.'

'Yes you do. Like lawyers and judges and stuff. If they write back you have to pay for their advice.'

And just at that moment I came across the matching paper and envelope set I got for my birthday. It was a sign!

So we go to the kitchen to write the letter to the Ombudsman, and we all have a banana smoothie with an extra scoop of ice-cream to give us ideas on what to say.

I write out the rough copy on the back of Zev's dad's computer paper. All of Stella Street writes on the back of Zev's dad's computer paper.

We all put in our ideas of what we think is important. We tell him about Rob and Donna being so nice, and the Phonies moving in and Briquette's banquet and how we cleaned up so fast and didn't leave a speck. And about the fence problem and everything at 47 being old and everything at 45 being new. And Briquette. Mostly about Briquette.

Then, on my birthday paper with the wattle and the blue wren in the corner of the page, in my neatest writing I do the good copy. It's three pages long. While I write Briquette leans on my foot as if she's helping me. The warmth of her dog's body is nice, and the rhythm of her panting.

When I finish we all sign the letter. Frank does a capital A in his name by mistake but we think it's better to leave it rather than rub it out and make it look scrubby.

We get the address out of the phone book and write it on the envelope in super neat writing. Then with a great flourish I lick the envelope.

'I am now going to make a wish,' I announce.

'Nobody makes wishes any more,' says Danielle who is a bit jealous of my beautiful letter. 'They're not true. That's just ancient namby-pamby garbage out of kiddie-winkies books. Anyway you have to have a spell or a fairy or something magic to help make your wish come true.'

'Well, how do you know that I haven't got something magic?'

'You have not,' says Danielle.

'How do you know?'

'You just haven't.'

'How do you know?'

'You haven't.'

'She has,' says Zev.

That surprised us all!

Frank comes to the rescue.

'And get Briquette to lick the stamp,' says Frank. 'She's got a lucky lick.'

'What?'

'Yep. Rob gets her to lick the stamp for important letters.'

So we sit Briquette up on a chair by the table.

'If she licks it, it will be a lucky lick and everything will work out all right,' says Frank.

Zev carefully holds the stamp up in front of Briquette's nose.

Briquette sits there panting with her usual idiot grin. For a second she sits there looking around, then she leans forward, as if she knows exactly what to do, and gives the stamp a big slobbery lick. It sticks to her tongue and she swallows it.

We all collapse laughing, and Briquette, the cause of all the trouble, sits looking around so pleased with herself.

We get another stamp and this time Zev hangs on to it. She licks it like a beauty.

Zev slaps the stamp on the envelope and we all march down to the letterbox and mail the letter. It slithers into the box and as I hear its papery landing, I silently make my wish. I think everybody else makes a wish too. Even Danielle who doesn't believe in wishes.

Dear God,
Can you please switch me through to St Francis of Assisi?

Dear St Francis, This is just not fair. Poor silly Briquette. She doesn't know any better. She's a dog. Can you please send a plague on the Phonies. It would be absolutely awful if Briquette has to have her bark removed. Everybody needs their voice. You're the patron saint of birds and animals. Can you please protect Briquette and dont let anything awful happen to her?

Henni

9

The new fence

This is what happened about the fence. Donna rang up the Phonies' solicitor and said Yes, a new fence would be OK, but they weren't going to pay all that cash, and she and Rob would build it.

Then Mr Smeeton wrote back saying his client didn't like that idea. Mr Smeeton's client preferred to use the fencing contractor who had already quoted.

Mr Smeeton's client wanted a proper job, not a fence 'of dubious quality'.

Then Donna rang Mr Smeeton again and outlined the fence they had in mind, materials, how long it would take and the cost, which, she pointed out, was much much much cheaper.

Then Mr Smeeton wrote back saying his clients weren't concerned about the cost.

Then Donna rang Mr Smeeton and said 'Lucky them', but Rob and Donna were concerned about the cost.

Then Donna sent him a drawing showing it was not going to be 'some failed freaky artistic statement' which is what the solicitor told Donna the Phonies had said. And she sent Mr Smeeton details about other things Rob had built. Finally the Phonies agreed to them building the fence.

One detail remained. The height of the fence.

Basically the Phonies wanted it twenty metres high with barbed wire and razor blades along the top. Just joking, but they did want it much higher.

Donna has firm ideas on fences. She loathes high fences.

She says they shut people in and shut people out and high front fences don't 'give to the street'. (47 sure gives to the street!) She says high fences are like someone wearing dark glasses all the time. As for the height of the side fence, she said, if it was any higher than the present fence she would feel like she was living in a prison.

There were more phone calls to Mr Smeeton. Donna never lost her temper. That's probably how she got the job she has. She never loses her temper. Rob would have told the Phonies to take a long walk off a short pier. Mum would have gone quiet. She just buttons up. Dad would have lost his temper, for sure, and called them inconsiderate pea brains. But not Donna. She just keeps on keeping on.

Eventually it was decided the height of the side fence would remain the same.

Donna sure got to know Mr Smeeton on the phone. Although he didn't say it, she could tell Mr Smeeton was getting fed up with the Phonies too.

Ever-patient Donna cleared away her garden that was beside the fence, lugging all the pots and containers round the back. She wanted to get it over with before the spring. At last there was nothing left beside the fence but the apricot tree and a couple of bushes. It looked as if everything else had fled before the battle.

Getting out the old fence was a breeze. Took about 45 seconds.

Rob was just saying, 'This'll last another 50 years.'

CCCC*RRRRRRRRRRASH!!!!!!* goes half the fence onto the Phonies' drive.

We had an A1 time building that new fence. We all helped. It was so cool. Some of the best times are building things or making things. Like a working bee when everyone helps. Like that part in 'Seven Brides for Seven Brothers' (one of Dad's favourite films) where they build a barn. I just love that bit.

The Phonies were away while the fence was built. Of course. They were represented by, yes you guessed it, good old Mr Smeeton. He turned up while we were sitting round eating carrot cake.

This car came crawling up the street and stopped opposite 45. This gawky guy was peering at us. Suddenly Donna jumps up.

'Mr Smeeton!' she cries and strides over to him. 'At last we meet!'

They shook hands. He had been instructed to check on the work. He was in a suit on a Saturday. He even had his camera. Donna and Mr Smeeton were like old chums.

Rob said, 'Great day for building fences.'

And Mr Smeeton, the wit, said 'That depends which side of the fence you're on!'

When he thawed out he was quite nice. He called around on Sunday wearing jeans and brought his wife and baby boy. Orchids were his passion and although there's a bit of difference between Donna's garden and orchids they got on famously.

Mr Nic is buzzing round happy as Looney Larry because he's getting enough firewood to warm his toes for the rest of winter.

He's singing knee-slapping, whoop-it-up Home in Texas songs, and he and Zev are carrying out old posts and planks to the footpath where Dad's cutting them up with the chainsaw he borrowed from a guy at work.

Dad's happy as Looney Larry too because he sits at a desk most days and here he's actually doing something. I mean doing something where you can see you've done something. He loves working with wood and never gets a chance.

Danielle and Frank are fetching this and finding that, when what should come on the radio but 'Check out the Exit'!

Danielle goes into her floppy-doll number, which stops the show. The oldies are amazed. They think it's fantastic.

Donna's happy. At last something's happening after all the letters and phone calls and stuff. One of life's problems solved.

Another of life's problems, Briquette, is happy. For her the Great Wall of China has come down. She's roaming around sniffing every square centimetre of Phonie territory.

For lunch we had messy meat pies with loads of sauce, sitting round where the fence used to be. Briquette, the greedy pig, watches every mouthful we take.

''Member how Old Auntie Lillie always had that enamel bowl of water beside the back step for Briquette,' says Dad softly scratching Briquette behind the ear.

''Member how she used to read the newspaper and say it was all bad news in the world today, and she was going to cancel the newspaper,' says Rob.

'She was going to cancel it for about fifteen years!' says Mr Nic.

''Member how she used to say "Goodness me!" '

We look across at what had once been home turf. Now it is enemy territory.

'She was a darling,' says Donna wistfully.

At first when we went into *their* space we stepped carefully as if landmines were about to blow us up. Then we got bolder. And we were like Briquette. Looking to see what we could see. Sniffing around...well...not actually sniffing around.

You know what I mean.

The lawn at the back of Old Auntie Lillie's house was gone. It's now paved, with expensive looking white garden furniture, and all round the edge of the paving instant rainforest busts out with built-in little sprinkler hoses keeping it tropical.

Frank dragged a garden chair up to the Phonies' side window to have a look inside.

'Come on. Don't be a perv,' said Dad. But we were all curious.

'Hey come and look at this!' yelled Danielle. 'It's like an art gallery.'

Well, that was it. Everybody wanted to have a look.

You could just see into the living room through a tiny gap between the sill and the blind. The room was dark. It was as you'd expect, absolutely clean and white. There was nothing that made them seem like normal people. No junk. They were living in a magazine house.

As for the paintings and the statues!!!!!!!!!!!!!!!!!!!!!!!!!!!!!!!!!
!!!
!!!
!!!!!!!!!!!!!!

Some of the paintings were in big crusty gold frames that make anything look important. You could stick a tracing of Garfield in one of those frames and people would say seriously deep things. There were lots of different sorts of paintings. Old ones. Modern ones. And a beautiful metal statue of a boy leading a horse, and a magnificent tall blue vase.

Mr Nic and Zev were the last to have a peep.

'WOWIE!!!' goes Zev. Without thinking he ran his fingers through his hair. Suddenly a piercing electronic scream hit the air. He set off the alarm! A bolt of panic shot through us. All the dogs in the neighbourhood went crazy, bark, bark, barking. It was awful. So shrill. Not just annoying...scary. Maria across the road, who was peeling potatoes, cut her finger.

Donna raced into 47 and rang good old Mr Smeeton.

'Something has accidentally set off the alarm at 45. It's making a terrible noise.'

Mr Smeeton apologised and said he'd be round immediately to turn it off. For, say, twenty minutes the shrilling went on.

At last Mr Smeeton arrived and turned it off. The silence was such a relief. But the mood had turned dark. We were all on edge.

Even though they weren't there the Phonies were still making our lives miserable.

We got back to the job but there was no joy in the fence building for the rest of the day.

10

Mr W.P. Burgess

Herr Hitler W. P. Burgess is the local dog catcher. Thick of body and dumb of head. He probably worked as a garbo for two weeks then he probably got a bad back and the Council pensioned him off into this job. Before that he was probably a not very good criminal and before that he was probably a punch swinger in a dumb but dangerous teenage gang, and before that he would have been the school bully. For sure.

He has a big red nose. He has a nasty temper and he doesn't like animals. He heaves up his dark blue trousers under his beer gut and clears his throat as if he has a shovelful of gravel in there.

'Mrs O'Sullivan I'm the Council dog catcher,' he says with pleasure. 'I'm here to warn you that we've had more complaints about your dog.'

Donna gave a long quiet sigh. 'Would you like to come in?'

'No thanks.'

'I guess it was our next-door neighbours?' Donna asks waving generally at 45.

'Yes,' said Burgess with a smug half-smile. 'They certainly complained very strongly, in no uncertain terms, but they weren't the only ones.'

Donna was surprised to hear others had complained as well. Most of Stella Street was on Rob and Donna's side.

'Yes. Your dog's been barking a lot. Early in the morning, late at night, and every time in between it seems,' says Mr Burgess his smug half-smile continuing.

Donna could see she wasn't going to win Bully Burgess over.

Explanations, excuses and arguments would only add to his satisfaction.

Briquette, who is inside the house, trots up to the front door to see what's going on.

Mr Burgess has left the gate wide open behind him.

Briquette lunges past Donna but Donna's too quick and grabs her up.

Briquette, in Donna's arms, can see that open gate, and wriggles, and wriggles and wriggles to get down and out that gate to 45.

'I'd advise you to give careful consideration to the future of that dog.'

'Now just what do you mean?' says Donna sharply.

'I'm just telling you the fines have recently gone up. If I catch that dog prowling round the streets hereabouts it's $150. That's what you're up for Mrs O'Sullivan. That's all I'm saying,' he says with a last self-satisfied hitch-up of his trousers.

11

The Ombudsman replies

All this time, when I arrived home from school every night, I checked out the mail for a letter from the Ombudsman. I was hoping desperately he would give us good advice, especially about Briquette, and then everything would be fine.

Frank told Rob we'd written to the omman's buddy.

At last, weeks later he replied.

With the compliments of

The Ombudsman

7th Floor, 412 George Street, Bellington, 3937 Australia
Tel: (03) 419 378 Fax: (03) 629 4883

Dear Henni, Zev, Danielle and Frank,

RE: 45 & 47 STELLA STREET

My job does not cover subjects like dogs or feuds between neighbours. My brief is to handle complaints about state and local government administration. There is a free telephone advice service. You can call Legal Aid at 607 0234.

Yours sincerely,

Robert Cooper

Robert Cooper
Ombudsman

P.S. I wish I could help you. Maybe there is someone living nearby who has a lot of experience and could give you some advice. I suggest you keep away from your neighbours and don't make trouble. Be guided by your parents. Incidentally it was a very good letter.

The bit in handwriting at the bottom of the letter made all the difference. He kept faith with me.

'Fat lot of help he is!' said Danielle. Next day I showed it to Zev and Frank.

'What about Briquette's lucky lick?' said Zev.

Frank looked gloomy. 'Maybe it's just not lucky any more,' he said sadly.

Briquette grinned up at us.

'Disappointment number five thousand and one,' said Danielle.

12

'Want to help me paint the fence?'

Donna, Donna
You'll get eaten.
They'll hand you in
to Mr Smeeton!

by Danielle

The first signs of life in her new garden really got Donna going again. Tinkering, planting, swapping stuff round, planning for spring. On fine mornings she was getting up before dawn so she could have a couple of hours in the garden before work.

'It's so beautiful. The garden at first light,' she said. 'All the little stirrings of life.'

There's Donna pottering in her old jumper and overalls, humming to herself, birds twittering, Briquette snuffling at her heels. Old Mr Sun peeping down in the early hours must have looked forward to spying this keen little person every morning.

The new fence looked so raw and new, especially beside their great old patched-up house. Donna studied the new fence from every angle, and consulted her flower books. One afternoon she came home from work with six colour cards of different paints, every colour of the rainbow.

'Mum's going to paint the new fence,' Frank announced next day.

'What colour?'

'Two colours,' he said.

*　　*　　*

When we took Frank home we asked Donna, 'What colour are you going to paint the fence?'

She showed us on a paint colour card. Rob was looking over her shoulder.

'Holy moly! You're crazy!' he said. 'You're just asking for trouble. The Phonies won't like it. I'm warning you. It will make them mad as hatters.'

'It's not their side of the fence,' said Donna. 'Anyway they're mad as hatters already!'

Rob said, 'All I know is that pink makes people mad.'

'It's not pink, it's magenta,' said Donna. 'It's such a happy colour. It's a fabulous colour. And near the front fence where all the daisies are I'm going to paint Greek blue.'

Donna stuck to her colours.

'Their side of the fence is their business. Our side of the fence is our business,' she said. 'It's only a fence after all!'

All us kids agreed with her. The colours she had picked were much much much more interesting than the boring old dark green or cream or brown that people usually paint fences.

'Go on, Mum,' says Frank. 'It'll look cool!'

'And I'm going to plant a purple bougainvillea by the magenta fence,' she said in a that-settles-that voice.

Rob scratched his head and said nothing.

* * *

Rob helped prepare the fence and undercoat it but when it came to the colour he disappeared. It was Donna and us kids. Cool fun.

We looked really sloppy in old sweaters and jeans. Donna had a scarf tied round her head like an old woman.

From the garage she heaved out two huge cans of paint. The outside of the can gave nothing away except the name of the paint—'Camille'. (Wonder what colour 'Henni' would be?) We spread out sheets of newspaper, then, with a big screwdriver Donna levered up the lid of the first can. The paint looked like oily milk.

'Needs a good stir,' she said.

We took it in turns to have fifty stirs of the paint, then we needed a rest because our arms ached. As we stirred the colour swirled up until it was like a thick rich cream. Magenta cream.

'Something's missing!' said Frank and disappeared into the house. He threw an extension cord out the kitchen window then reappeared with the tape recorder and plugged it in. Gypsy Kings boomed out across the backyard.

'This is the music for this colour!' he said.

Danielle's doing a gypsy dance.

Needless to say the Phonies were away.

We spread out old curtains at the foot of the fence, then the fun began. The paint went on like melted butter.

'Who could hate this colour!' said Donna. 'It's the colour of holidays.'

'Flowers,' said Frank.

'Sunsets on desert islands,' I said.

'Dancing costumes,' said Danielle.

'Briquette's tail!' said Zev. 'What a clown!'

She grinned up at us, furiously wagging a tail with a pink tip.

It was just as well there were two big cans of paint because quite a lot of it didn't make it onto the fence. It was on us, the apricot tree, on the ground, on the old curtains, Frank's arms, etc, etc, etc.

Claire from down the road did some painting too, until she had to go to work. She's a nurse.

Mr Nic turned up. He had been to a funeral. He was wearing his good clothes so he sat himself on a kitchen stool a long way from the action. Briquette couldn't understand why he didn't want to know her.

He said, 'That colour reminds me of a dress.'

Then he wouldn't say what dress.

Lunch was pizza delivered, and a banana whiz with big scoops of chocolate ice-cream.

We transformed that fence. It was a work of art. We painted the blue part last. It was the colour of a deep blue sky.

Rob turned up just as we finished.

'Wow!' said Rob taking it all in. 'There's only one thing missing, the words "WELCOME HOME PHONIES!"'

Donna gave him a shove.

* * *

That evening Donna, Rob and Frank came round to our place for supper.

I heard Donna telling Mum, 'It's OK on good days when I wake up feeling strong. I just think what stupid intolerant twits we're living next to. But on bad days it gets me down. Briquette's a real worry.'

And I heard Rob telling Dad, 'All I know is she's stuck to her guns about that colour. And she's usually the sensible one. Maybe it's her way of hitting back. They're stupid jerks you know. I had to park in front of their house the other day. There was no space out the front of our place. And when I came back there was a whacking great sign on the truck windscreen—DO NOT PARK HERE! As if they own the street! Territorial idiots!

'And last week I pruned the plum tree and put the prunings in the back lane till I could load them up and take them to Val for kindling. Suddenly the prunings are back in our yard. Someone's heaved them back over the fence. Three days later, blow me down, there's a solicitor's letter from good old Mr Smeeton saying please do not leave prunings in the back lane, they might scratch his client's car.'

* * *

Yep! Rob was right. Definitely. One thing you can say about the Phonies—they're reliable. If there's something to complain about, they'll complain.

The Phonies just loved Donna's pink. One look at it and they saw ***RED!***

It took only five days from when we painted the fence for the solicitor's letter to arrive complaining about the colours.

It was from a new solicitor this time, Mr J.D. Perry. Maybe Mr Smeeton wasn't tough enough. Maybe his heart wasn't in his job. Maybe he told the Phonies to shove off. Maybe he wasn't expensive enough. Who knows.

Once again through a solicitor's letter, the Phonies taught us what you can and can't do. We had no idea there were rules about what colour you can and can't paint your house and stuff, but it seems Donna had broken some planning law.

And Mr Perry made it very clear.

PERRY SOLICITOR

P O Box 1311 Glenwood 3779 T 7499111 F 749198

Mr & Mrs O'Sullivan
47 Stella Street
Bakers Hill

Dear Sir/Madam,

RE: External Paint Colours - Fence at 47 Stella Street

I wish to advise you that, on instruction from my clients, the following has been brought to the notice of the Barrima Council.

1. With the introduction of Statutory Urban Conservation Controls, owners are required to make application to Council with regard to paint colours for large external areas.

2. (a) The paint colours you have used do not accord with the objectives of Clause 25L of the Bakers Hill Planning Scheme.

(b) The paint colours are not in harmony with the existing character and appearance of the area.

(c) Approval of such colours would jeopardise the proper future development of the locality as a Statutory Urban Conservation Area.

3. Should the owners subsequently challenge Council's decision by ...ing an appeal with the Administr... Appeals Tribunal (A.A.T)

bla bla bla bla

Donna didn't have much success trying to phone Mr Perry. He was a very busy man, either in a meeting or on another call, or he'd just gone out. Donna left message after message but he never rang back.

We christened Mr Perry, Mr Slippery.

13

The new new car

UPDATE! UPDATE! UPDATE!

You know the Phonies had a new car, a silver one. It was a Bentley turbo. Smooth and elegant. Well folks, something must have been wrong with it. Must have had an imperfection. Must have been a hair on the seat, or maybe a speck of dust on the steering wheel. We don't want to be bothered with a speck of dust do we daaaaaahlings? Anyway that car's gone.

They've got a new car. It's a Mercedes Benz S Class. We saw them gliding off in their new grey slug. Actually we *think* we saw them gliding off. It's got dark windows so you can't see who's inside, but unfortunately we think it's still them.

We rang up the car dealer.

'I'm inquiring about a Mercedes Benz,' Zev asks in his man-on-the-radio voice.

'New or used?' asks reception.

'Oh *must* be new,' says Zev, and gets switched through to the salesman.

'Good afternoon, Sir, may I help you?'

'We are thinking of buying a new car,' says Zev. 'What would it cost to purchase a new Mercedes S Class 600 with all the extras?'

He said, 'All the bells and whistles, Sir?'

Sir says, 'Yes please, an S Class 600 with the works.'

Salesman, 'In round figures that would be $356,000.'

Sir says, 'Thank you my good man, we'll have four of them!' and hangs up.

$356,000 for a car! Just to move their bodies around.

Zev said, 'That's worth two houses!'

How could they spend so much money on so little fun? It didn't even look fantastic. No sleek fins. No great shape. No TV. No spa bath. No doughnut machine. No Nintendo. No drink dispenser. Just a boring-looking two tons of metal.

'But,' says Zev, 'with a car like that you will never have to actually walk anywhere and you will never have to bump into undesirables...'

'Like us, for example,' I add.

'...and you don't have to actually speak to the unspeakable neighbours on the footpath...'

'Like us, for example.'

'...you just glide on by.'

Think of what you could do with all that money.

We were dead keen to know what was wrong with the old new car.

14

Bully Burgess strikes

Rob arrives home. Sits down. Has a cup of tea. It's quiet. Something's missing. Where's the dog! ***Briquette?*** Goes out to the backyard. ***Briquette? Briquette?*** No galloping little black dog's body. ***Briquette? Briquette? Briquette?*** Shut herself in the shed again? No. Rob does a tour of the fence. No signs of digging. No holes in the fence. Nothing. No sign of escape. ***Briquette? Briquette? Briquette?***

Donna arrives home from work and we arrived home from school with Frank.

In their anger, worry and fear for Briquette, Rob and Donna are yelling at each other. We've never seen them yelling like this before.

'When I left the front gate was shut. Did *you* shut the front gate?'

'I *always* shut the front gate!'

'So do I *always* shut the front gate!'

'Well she got out, didn't she!'

'What do you think happened?'

'Well, what do *you* think happened?'

'Hell, I don't know what happened!'

Donna stopped. 'Look. We both shut the front gate. We've been shutting the front gate for years. Maybe we left it open today, but I doubt it.'

Rob and Donna fell silent.

Up and down the streets we go. ***Briquette? Briquette?***

But no little black dog. Claire and Mrs Virgo from down the street are looking too. Briquette knows Stella Street so well how could she go missing? It's never happened before. Our imagination runs wild. We're looking under cars and behind bins and bushes, half afraid of what we might find. It's awful. If you've ever mislaid a pet you will understand.

Rob goes back to the house to get his bike so he can search further afield, and hears the phone ringing. It's Bully Burgess, the dog catcher. Of course we'd all thought about him, but he was last on our list.

'We've got your dog, Mr O'Sullivan. Come down to the pound and collect her.'

Everyone heaved a huge sigh of relief. Down to the Council dog pound we go and there's Briquette lying in a cage by herself. Her long nose is stretched forward, head on her paws, ears down, eyes soulful. She's absolutely miserable, and pathetic.

The second she sees us she's a barking, jumping, tail-wagging blur of happiness.

So Rob pays $150 and we take her home. Briquette was ecstatic to be free and delighted by all the fuss.

'Did they give you a warning?' asked Mum. 'You know—This time we'll overlook it. Don't let it happen again.'

'What do you think?' says Donna. 'Would Bully Burgess let his own mother off? No fear. He charged us the full $150.' She sighed. 'There goes my sewing machine repair money.'

'Bloody dog,' says Rob. 'So what do we do now? Put a lock on the front gate? We can't keep forking out $150. Only the Phonies have that sort of cash.'

It crossed our minds that certain people could easily have opened the gate just long enough to let a certain dog out.

We couldn't be sure. But it crossed all our minds.

15

A gift of a day

'Right!' says Dad.

When he says 'Right!' like that, something is going to happen. Or else.

'We've had enough of this,' he says. 'We're being battered by these idiots. We need cheering up. What are we doing next Sunday?' He slings on his jacket.

'Nothing!' Mum yells after him as he strides out the door.

After an hour and probably four cups of tea he's back.

'It's all organised. We're going to Splitter's Beach for a picnic next Sunday. Rob and Donna, Sue and Tibor, us and Val.' (Mr Nic)

Good old Dad, I thought. He's dead right we need cheering up.

Mum says, 'Bit of a risk isn't it, Splitter's in winter? Could be dismal if it's cold.'

'No worries,' says Dad. 'I've put in an order. Sunny. Twenty-two degrees. Light breeze. Mild surf. Clear blue sky.'

* * *

Monday: Freezing. Bucketing down rain.

Tuesday: Bitter cold. Pelting with rain.

Wednesday: Freezing. Gales. Horizontal rain.

Thursday: Bitter. Pelting horizontal, vertical and oblique rain. Floods in the east.

Friday: Coldest day for 23 years. More rain.

Saturday: Milder and clearing showers.

Sunday: You guessed it! There was no rain left in the sky.

* * *

The tide is out at Splitter's when we arrive. Lazy waves of pale blue glass take their turn to break, then slide up and tickle the shore. The beach is absolutely washed clean. There are four puffs of white cloud in the very bluest of blue skies.

We have forgotten what blue sky looks like.

In the middle of the smooth wide mirror of wet sand Danielle turns cartwheels, then flings her arms out and whirls and whirls around until she crashes down dizzy.

We have the beach to ourselves.

Briquette bursts out of the car racing down the beach, skittering huge circles in the sand, yapping and bounding and going crazy like a puppy, flattening her ears back, stretching out her tail doing her mad run. She runs like this when she is deliriously happy. She gets a silly kink in her tail. We know exactly how she feels. The beach made us all feel free.

Coolers and baskets and blankets come out of the cars. We spread ourselves. Mr Nic is handing round bottles of his home brew, telling the most pathetic jokes. His jokes are so lame, and he tells them so badly, we are all in stitches of laughter.

Dad produces his favourite sausages, from the man at the market who sells 62 sorts of sausages including crocodile, emu, kangaroo, and (Rob reckons) dog, cat, lizard, possum, snake, bandicoot, gumboot, tractor tire, etc, etc, etc.

Donna produces her famous industrial-strength banana cake with a thick slathering of fantastic soft chocolate icing.

'Can I lick all the icing off?' says Frank.

'You *ate* half the icing when we made the cake,' laughs Donna.

Zev wriggles his toes in the sand with his eyes closed and a smile of bliss. He's been wearing new hiking boots and three pairs of socks. Bare feet. Cool silky sand between bare toes. Warm sun soaking through jumpers onto white winter skin. Oh joy! Oh happiness! Oh glorious delight!

The adults lie around on blankets, empty beer and wine bottles on the grass looking like the end of a drinkers' orgy. Nothing moving except their lips.

Donna was using Rob's bare back as a pillow, with his tee-shirt draped over her face.

It reminded me of once we went to the zoo on a sunny day in winter and all the animals had spread themselves out, draped over rocks like washing drying, catching every possible ray of sun.

Briquette was in seventh heaven. She checked out all the garbage cans, found a month-old, half-eaten barbecue lamb chop, and chewed it for ages, then flaked out in the sun. A seagull landed near her. She opened one eye a slit and looked at the seagull.

She thinks 'Will I chase it or not?' She shuts her eye again. Now that's relaxed!

And the adults were like that too. Every now and then I'd catch a word or two.

We were making sand castles. I could just hear bits of conversation drifting over and lovely cackles of laughter.

'...beats me...where do they get it all from?...does he strike you as earning an honest dollar?...fanatical dame...thank God they didn't reproduce...charismatic?...would *you* send *them* money?...'

No prizes for guessing who they were talking about.

Then we all made cars, pushing the sand up around us. Making these hot car noises we had this hilarious beach Grand Prix. (I must stop staying 'this'. It always happens when the words start galloping! Oh too bad!)

Then Rob came down and put on his crash helmet which was a limpet, shook hands with us all, waved to the crowd, and built this huge sort of Batmobile around himself which we called the Robmobile.Then he acted like he was driving at a million kilometres an hour and suddenly had a terrible accident and was flung out of his car and lay dead.

But Donna said he still won and presented him with this huge wreath of wet seaweed which she dumped on him. Suddenly he came alive and chased her right to the other end of the beach where she pushed him in.

It was one of those glorious dopey days. Danielle began a collection of treasures, mostly pieces of glass that had been worn smooth on the rocks, shells, pieces of sea anemones and a Japanese cork. There were lots of shells with holes. They fitted on our fingers but broke easily. We were bumping into each other and swapping them and saying 'I divorce you', 'Will you marry me?'

You know what it's like when you go to the beach. You go for a paddle and your clothes get wet so you go for a swim. The water was absolutely freeeeeezing, direct from the Antarctic, straight up the left hand side of Tasmania.

It was almost worth being frozen solid, when we climbed into the back seat of a warm stuffy car that had been locked up in the sun all day. We had to sit on our towels because the seat was so hot.

On the way home we all stopped for fish and chips as the sun set in a blaze over the silver sea and all that poetic stuff. We felt so happy. Somehow those people we won't mention were totally unimportant. We sang most of the way home.

Frank fell asleep on my shoulder, and some of the silly songs we sang reminded me of kindergarten days when life was simple.

'What a gift of a day,' said Dad.

16

Accused!

It was a week later on Monday morning at the break. I saw Zev walking straight towards me. He still had the easy walk but he waved his arm giving me a kind of stop signal. He has the sort of face that's nearly smiling all the time but there was something strange about it this day. He grabbed my arm.

'Quick. Come to the science room. I've got something to tell you.'

The room was quiet. We sat in the corner near the fish tank. Zev leant forward, half whispering.

'Somebody tried to burn down the Phonies' and they think it was us.'

'*Wowie zowie* you're *joking!*' I picked my ears up off the floor.

'I wish I was.'

'*True?*'

'True!'

'Henni, somebody stuffed old rags and bundles of paper under their back door and poured gas on it and dropped a match.'

'*You're kidding?* I can't *believe* it. Did it burn much?'

'It burnt the bottom of the door, the steps and part of the back wall and wrecked their hot-water service and the Phonies are stark, blazing, crazy, hopping mad and they are *positive* we did it.'

'*WHAT?*...That's stupid. When are we supposed to have done it?'

'Sunday evening—last night.'

'That's crazy. We were...what were we doing?'

'We were playing Spotlight, Henni. We're in hot water.'

'Oh gosh.'

My heart sank through my shoes into the middle of the earth.

Some kids came into the science room.

'We can't talk here!' says Zev. 'Tell Danielle. I've got to go!'

But I couldn't tell Danielle because Mum had collected her from school to go to the dentist.

* * *

Late Sunday afternoon we had taken a plant around to Granny Pembroke's for Donna. She's an old friend who lives in Aberfeldy Street which is about ten minutes away.

We came home by the park and there we met three of the Brown Boys, Wayne, Jason and Chris. Nobody trusts the Brown Boys they're always in so much trouble. When they're playing soccer it's different. Everyone's cheering for them at soccer because they take risks and play really hard and exciting. But you don't just turn off the wild side and suddenly be nice polite well-behaved boys. Not if you're a Brown Boy.

They're wild but they're OK. Mum and Dad have never actually said, 'You must not play with the Brown Boys', but I sort of understand they don't want us to have anything much to do with them. Some kids are scared of the Brown Boys. I feel sorry for them because teachers and adults pick on them all the time, and sometimes it's not their fault—but usually it is.

Chris Brown was looking for possums with a big new flashlight. It had a fantastic beam so we played Spotlight. It was the perfect night for it, except if you were supposed to be somewhere else.

Spotlight is this cool game we played at school camp. You need a dark night. You need a place like a park with plenty of space but little bushes and things here and there. You need a few kids and a good flashlight.

One person is 'IT' in the middle of the space with the flashlight. They're only allowed to snap on the light for a second. And you sneak up to them. If you reach them you're 'IT'. They listen in the dark and if they hear you, the beam of light snaps out to catch you.

It's a dark, silent and very exciting game. You hear all the sounds of the night. Every croak and creak, crackle and rustle. Some people play it like commandos and make sudden mad dashes. I like to go slowly, with stealth, slithering, keeping low, not sticking to the trees and bushes, lying flat in the open where they don't expect you.

It gets dark so early in winter.

That's what we were doing on Sunday night, when we had promised to come straight home.

* * *

After school I had netball practice. I played badly. I kept dropping the ball. I was dreading going home. Thank goodness Danielle had to go to the dentist. That usually means a lot of waiting around so I knew Mum and Danielle would be late getting back. I knew Dad would be home late because he had gone to Sydney.

As soon as I got in the door Mum said in a strained voice, 'Henni, they want you and Danielle down at the police station for questioning about a fire at the Phonies'.' She stood looking at me. 'What have you kids done?'

'Mum, nothing bad, honestly. Nothing!'

It was nearly dark. Driving there someone flashed their headlights bright in Mum's eyes because she hadn't put her lights on. We sat in the car each lost in our own headful of worries.

As we arrived at the police station Sue, Tibor and Zev, and Donna, Rob and Frank were coming out. No happy smiles. No friendly jokes. Solemn faces. Donna looked tired and worn. I felt especially sorry for Tibor who looked grey and old. He shook his head and said, 'I came to Australia so I wouldn't have anything more to do with police stations.' He is the kindest, gentlest man. What did he mean?

'Come to our place afterwards,' Tibor said as we went in.

At the front counter of the police station there were posters of criminals and awful photographs of people missing. From these old grey photos you knew they were already dead. It was all cold and hard and very scary.

'Mrs Octon?' the policeman at the counter asked. He had a thick black belt with half a ton of police gadgets on it, including a gun which you just couldn't help looking at. He picked up the phone and called someone. 'The two girls are here for you Dave.' Turning back to us. 'Won't be a moment.'

Detective Sergeant Dave Watson introduced himself. He was wearing a sharp grey suit instead of a police uniform. He looked at Danielle, me and Mum and wrote in a big book details of who we were, what time it was, and what it was about.

'Follow me,' he said, and led us down a corridor of shiny lino past battered lockers, signs and noticeboards, past desks in rooms, round bends. The only cheerful thing I saw was a sports calendar. We had to go in single file because the corridor was narrow. At last we were shown into a small blank room. There was a battered wooden desk and a few worn black office chairs. The ceiling was low and there wasn't a colour in the room. It was all grey. The only different thing was a strange tape recorder. If you had to think of the opposite of Donna's garden, this was it.

Detective Sergeant Watson sat Danielle and me down close to the table so he could record what we said. The tape recorder, which was a large shiny silver box, made three copies at the same time. Mum was sitting beside Danielle. He shut the door and set the recorder going.

First Watson said to the recorder what it was all about then he leaned forward to Danielle.

'Now Danielle, tell me everything that happened on Sunday afternoon.'

'We went to Granny Pembroke's. She's a friend. We took her a plant from our friend Donna.'

'How long were you at Granny Pembroke's?'

Danielle looked at me, then back to Watson.

'Ages.'

I felt hot and sick. I didn't know whether to interrupt and say she was lying, because she knew we'd done the wrong thing.

He wanted to know what time we met. Whose idea was it? Which way we went? What happened? What did we see on the way?

The tape was rolling the whole time. I could just see the reels moving and Danielle's lies being recorded three times over.

'...then we said, "Goodbye. See you next week" and came home.' This was after Danielle had invented afternoon tea with sponge cake and a look at some of Granny Pembroke's old photos and the ivory fan with a picture of a whale on it ...which I realised was exactly what had happened the last time we went round to see Granny Pembroke.

'Did you come straight home?'

'Yes,' said Danielle looking at me again.

'Thank you Danielle,' said Watson.

Mum was sitting straight in her chair with her hands clenched tightly. She looked so pathetic. It wasn't fair. I felt so awful that we all had to go through this. I felt ablaze with fury at the Phonies. It was all their fault somehow or other.

'This is what really happened,' I said in a loud clear voice so the recorder could hear every word.

'We went round to Granny Pembroke's, but we were there for only about five minutes because she was going out. We delivered the plant, had a little chat and left. Danielle told you exactly what happened when we visited Granny Pembroke about two weeks ago.'

'Oh I forgot!' says Danielle. Then she jumps up, stumps her hands on her hips, and goes off like a cork exploding. 'What about the Phonies? Ask them about Briquette! Everybody hates their stinking guts! We wish they'd been burnt to the ground and them sizzled up and gone to hell. But we just *WISH* that. We wouldn't ever *DO* it!'

Mum gently folded her arms around Danielle and sat her on her knee. Danielle was making all these strange faces that I knew were fighting-back-the-tears faces.

But Danielle would rather die than cry.

Detective Sergeant Watson gave Danielle a long look. Despite the faces she was pulling Danielle was looking him straight in the eye.

He turned to me.

'So, Henni. Where were you between the hours of 6 pm and 8 pm last night?'

'We were playing a game in the park.'

'In the dark?' says Watson. 'You can play this game in the dark?'

'Yes,' I said, 'it's called Spotlight. You try and catch people in the spot of a flashlight.'

'So you had a flashlight?'

'Yes.'

'Was it yours?'

'No.'

'Was this Zev's flashlight?'

'No.'

(What had the others told him? What did he know? I didn't know who knew what.)

'Your sister's light?'

'No.'

'Well whose flashlight was it?'

I was stuck. I didn't want to say the Brown Boys.

'I don't know.'

The minute I said that, I knew I'd made a blunder. I was lying and he knew it and I knew it. He looked me straight in the eyes and I couldn't look back.

'I see,' he said.

'Now how many of you were playing this Spotlight?'

'Zev and Danielle and me and Frank... Oh, and the Brown Boys. Actually I've remembered it was Chris Brown's light.'

'So it was Chris Brown's flashlight?'

'Yes.'

'Now are you sure you were all there all the time?'

'Yes.'

'But wouldn't it be hard to tell, in the dark, if someone wasn't there.'

'No we were all there.'

'You played this game Spotlight for about how long?'

'I don't know. Maybe an hour.'

'Now you left Granny Pembroke's round 6.15 and you played this game for an hour and you got home round 8 o'clock, and you say that's an hour?'

'Well... it's hard to tell when you're playing Spotlight.'

Mum, who hadn't said a word until now leaned forward with a sharp edge to her voice.

'This is sounding like a court case.'

'I'm sorry Mrs Octon. I'm just trying to clarify a couple of points.'

He turned to me again.

'Did anyone see you, or did you see anyone else in the park, or on the way home from the park?'

I desperately tried to think of someone or something but I couldn't.

'No. Not that I can remember.'

Again and again he asked me questions about the game, his eyes staring into me. What happens in the game? Who was

'IT' first? Was Zev ever 'IT'? Was Zev near you? Where was Frank? What was the flashlight like? What was the result of the game?

At last he stopped.

'OK Henni.' He turned off the tape.

He looked at his watch, sat back and crossed his arms. You could see by the strange way his suit folded there was something under his arm. It was probably his gun. He spoke deliberately looking hard at me.

'The Brown Boys said they were at the Davies' place, and Mr Davies says they were.' He paused to let that sink in. 'And we found this at the scene of the fire.'

There, sealed up in a plastic bag, with a label on it, was Zev's smooth red comb. Bent from heat. Unmistakable.

'For everybody's sake, young lady, I think you'd better get your story straight.'

Here's the awful thing.

For a flash of a second I thought maybe Zev did race back and burn the Phonies. But that was impossible. He would *never* do that. What on earth was I doing thinking like that? Besides he was playing Spotlight with us.

But when this detective started suggesting things, with his cunning questions and sitting there with his gun under his arm and his bullet eyes boring into me I started to doubt the facts.

'We'll be in touch Mrs Octon. We'll need to bring them back in for further questioning.'

17

No alibi

When we got to Zev's everyone was sitting around the old kitchen table on chairs and stools. The others had collected a couple of pizzas on the way home. I was starving.

'Great way to spend a Monday evening,' said Donna. 'Down at the police station, having a detective interview your kids.'

'Have some pizza,' said Sue.

Poor Dad arrived at last after reading the note we left on the kitchen table. It was early in the morning when he left for Sydney and now he looked beat. He had a splitting headache. Sue gave him an aspirin.

He heard the whole sorry business. He groaned when the Brown Boys came into the story.

'This is *PREPOSTEROUS!*' he said with his head in his hands.

'What's that mean?' whispered Frank.

'Something bad,' said Zev.

Sue was wringing her hands off her wrists, '...and so exasperating!'

I knew that one.

'It means it makes you mad!' I told the other kids.

Everybody felt angry.

We all knew what the parents were going to say and they knew what we were going to say but somehow everybody just had to say it all.

'You were supposed to come straight home. You *promised*, remember?'

'We were going to, but it was such a great night.'

'You know you're not supposed to be wandering around in the dark by yourselves.'

'But we weren't on our own, and we weren't wandering. There were seven of us and you can only play Spotlight at night with a few people...'

'...and we never get to play Spotlight.'

'You've been warned about staying out in the evenings.'

'But it wasn't cold. Actually it was the best game of Spotlight.'

Then we got the old 'Can't we trust you any more?'.

'But we didn't really do anything wrong.'

'Now about the Brown Boys...'

'They're not that bad,' I said.

'You *know* they're trouble! You've been *warned* about the Brown Boys.'

'You haven't actually *said* we mustn't play with them. How were we to know that?'

'I heard they got a last warning about something that happened down at Time Zone,' said Mum.

'That would explain it,' said Tibor. 'If they're in trouble already, they don't want more trouble.'

'They didn't do anything wrong,' said Frank.

'Would everyone believe that?' said Dad.

'Well, you've learnt one thing,' said Donna. 'Don't bank on the Brown Boys.'

We all felt a bit better after a spot of yelling and some pizza.

Zev and Frank had both told the truth. One funny thing was that Frank's stomach had rumbled so loudly he made Watson smile, and we all laughed about the police listening to it when they played back the tape.

We told about Danielle's fable, then her outburst. She was putting on lots of bravo but I knew what it had really been like. It wasn't funny at all.

Mum said, 'Watson was fascinating as he listened to the girls' version. You'd never know he'd heard the story before.'

'For a plain-clothes detective I thought his plain-clothes were pretty snappy,' said Donna.

'Are you children *sure* you didn't see anyone else at the park?' asked Sue.

'You'd be OK if you had a good alibi.'

'What's an alibi?' whispered Frank.

'Someone who was with you somewhere else, when the crime happened.'

'Can't you think of *anyone* you saw at the park who could say they saw you there?'

'Can a dog be an alibi?' said Frank. 'I patted a labrador.'

'No alibi!' said Zev.

The talk swung around from the events at the police station to guessing about what happened at the Phonies'.

The amazing thing was that none of us were in Stella Street at the time of the fire. Rob and Donna had taken Mum and

Dad to an exhibition opening of a painter friend of Donna's, and Sue and Tibor were visiting Sue's old aunt in hospital.

The alarm was raised by the Neales, the neighbours on the other side. The Phonies arrived as the firefighters were packing up.

'Don't you wish you'd been there when the cops and the fire-fighters were talking to the Phonies!' said Dad.

'Wonder if they're interviewing the Phonies in depth? I sure would like to!' said Rob.

'They're such ambassadors for peace and happiness they've probably got dozens of close friends who would love to do them in,' said Tibor.

'You know something,' said Donna, talking to herself, 'I don't think I've ever seen the mailman deliver them a letter.'

'I bet Mrs P turned on her charm,' said Zev.

'...like a fire hose!' said Frank.

'Why did they have to come and live in Stella Street? Why didn't they buy a mansion out in North Boring?' said Danielle.

'What about the red comb, Zev?'

'I lost it a couple of weeks ago.'

'They didn't find any fingerprints or footprints?'

'What about bits of rag or matches or cigarette lighter or whatever?'

'Not that we know about.'

'What do we do?' said Donna. 'Do we all chip in for a private detective and pay him big bucks to find out what really happened?'

'We do nothing,' said Rob. 'Just sit tight. I think Watson probably has a fair idea of what went on with our kids. The police sure have a clear picture of our relationship with the Phonies!' He gave Danielle a sad smile.

'Well it's late now,' said Tibor. 'Tomorrow is another working day. Off you go home.' He shooed us out like chickens.

'Maybe we trust our kids too much,' said Tibor.

'I don't think so,' said Dad.

There were hugs of solidarity all round.

* * *

Next day I tackled the Brown Boys.

'How was it?' asked Wayne.

'We got shafted,' I said.

'Yeah well, we've got our own problems,' said Chris. (Mum was right.)

'We're good boys now,' said Wayne. 'We stay right out of trouble.'

I laid it on Wayne Brown. 'You sneaky rats. You should have said you were playing Spotlight with us. Now they think we're lying.'

'What do you want me to do?' says Wayne. 'Go to the cops and say we were playing games with the goodie-goodies?'

'I hate your guts!' I said.

'I love you too, Shorty!' said Chris.

'Remember this,' I said. 'You really owe us one.'

'Great game of Spotlight wasn't it!' Chris yelled after me as I walked away down the street.

I trudged home from school so miserable.

Dear God,

You know how you say the meek will inherit the earth — the meek are <u>not</u> inheriting the earth. The meek are being done like a dinner. Please do something to help the meek.

Yours in need,

Henni

One of the meek.

18

'Ve haf vays of makink you talk!'

Wednesday night after school was the first chance we had to get together after the fateful Sunday. What a mess we were in. The worst trouble of our lives. But the funny thing is, you can't stay glum for ever.

Danielle was cheery and cheeky and we caught her madness.

She started jumping on the bed singing

> *'Oh Heck! We're in a mess.*
> *Guess I'd better catch a bus!'*

'That's pathetic!' said Zev whacking her on the head with a pillow. 'Mess and bus don't even rhyme.'

> *'Sizzle up the Phonie witch.*
> *She's so rich.*
> *Give her the stitch.'*

So then there's a pillow fight and we're all yelling at Danielle to shut up.

'Hey slow down,' said Mum bringing in a big plate of soft spongy white bread ham sandwiches which are my favourite. When I saw those sandwiches I knew Mum believed us, and I loved her so much.

We were ravenous. Silence (except for the sound of chewing).

> *'I've got Phonies up my chimney'*

'SHUT UP DANIELLE!'

'What happened at your place?' I asked Zev.

'Not much,' he said. 'What about you?'

'Same. I thought we were going to be in for terrible trouble. I thought we'd be grounded, no TV, no treats, no pocket-money, the works.'

'No showers, no sneezing, no Nutella, no air...'

'SHUT UP DANIELLE!'

'Mum and Dad are worried, but nothing's banned and we're not grounded.'

'How's Rob and Donna, Frank?'

'O...K...' said Frank slowly. 'They're not very happy.'

'Seriously though, Rob was right,' says Zev. 'We don't know *anything* about the Phonies. We don't know who they are and what they do.'

'My new car is a submarine.'

'SHUT UP DANIELLE!'

'So how do we find out about them?'

'Hook them up to a lie detector!' says Danielle.

'What's a lie detector?' asks Frank.

'Well, it's a machine. They put little wires on you and they ask you questions, and when you reply they watch a little needle on a meter, and if you're lying the reading is high. If you're telling the truth it's low. I think it's based on your heart beat. Like this!'

I grab Briquette and wind my skipping rope round her.

She's wriggling like crazy.

'Now just stay still Mr Phonie, while we ask you some questions. Mr Phonie, did you burn your own house down and blame it on us?'

'Aff! Aff!'

'Reading one thousand. I thought so.'

'Did you drop my comb so we would get blamed?' says Zev.

'Aff! Aff! Aff! Aff!'

'Reading two thousand. Just as I thought!'

'Do you chew your wife's jewels?' asked Frank.

'Aff! Aff! Aff! Aff!'

'Reading three thousand!'

By now Mr Phonie has the lie detector wrapped around his tail and is so wriggly, excited and tangled in the lie detector he's half biting us.

'I think we can no longer be sure that the answers are accurate,' I say.

'Thank you Mr Phonie, you may go.'

'I don't think the Phonies will lie still either,' said Danielle.

'Well, we could ask them questions,' said Frank slowly.

'Yeah sure, Frank. How?' I said.

'We could say it's for a school project,' said Frank.

'You and your school projects!' we all said. 'You've never even *done* one.'

'Questionnaires!' said Danielle. 'Like that lady who came around and asked Dad all those things about cars that time. You just knock on their door and say, 'Excuse me, I'm from Bla Bla Bla. I'll just take a few minutes of your time. Do you use Bla Bla Bla? What do you think of Bla Bla Bla? Then you just keep asking them questions like crazy.'

'Not possible. They would be totally suspicious,' I said.

'Disguise!' said Danielle.

'You're kidding.'

'No honestly!' says Danielle. 'You figure out some questions and I'll get disguised. Give me five minutes.'

So we drew up a list of questions.

1 What do you have for breakfast?

2 What is your favourite song?

3 What sort of work do you do?

4 Do you like peanuts? etc, etc, etc.

Danielle comes back wearing the brown curly wig out of the dress-up box, my jeans and my blue jumper. She did look different, especially her mouth.

'Danielle, what have you done to your mouth?'

She pulled a green string bean from under her top lip and another from her bottom lip.

'Great isn't it! They do it like this in Hollywood. Dustin Hoffman had beans under his lips for a whole movie!'

'Was it the same beans all the time?' asked Frank.

She tested the questionnaire out on Mr Nic. It went beautifully. He answered every question with great consideration, but then he is always so polite and helpful. Besides, he didn't have his glasses on.

We decided Danielle and I would try the questionnaire a couple of streets away. I am tall and when I put make-up on I look older.

Our story was that we were students earning extra money. We knocked on two doors before we got a customer.

wig
bean
bean

The bean disguise

sideways view

A woman in a dressing-gown. At first we went fine. I jotted down her answers and started to get interested in what she was saying. She kept asking 'Who is it for again?'

Danielle was doing really well with the questions, then disaster!

The green bean in her top lip slipped!

The lady was immediately suspicious.

'She's got green gum disease,' I said. 'We'd better go.'

'Yes, you'd better,' says the woman crossing her arms.

We walked to the corner, then raced home screaming with laughter.

It was a dismal flop.

'Seriously though. What will we do?' said Zev.

We decided to each have a think and talk about it at Frank's next day.

* * *

We were mucking around in Frank's room. Frank, who'd been to swimming lessons, was combing his wet hair forward to look like a goodie and back to look like a baddie. Danielle got into the act swishing her hair luxuriously like the girl in the shampoo commercial.

Zev went straight to the point.

'We spy,' he said.

'Spy how? What do you mean, spy?'

'Just spy on them, you twit.'

'Gosh.'

'Why do they want a satellite dish? What do they watch? Where do they go all the time? Where do they get all the money? Why do they have parties?'

The rest of us sat there listening. He was dead serious.

'We get close to them and we watch them, and we write it down so we remember it all.'

Author's note: We never wrote down a thing.

19

Operation 'Night Eye'

Boy this was reckless. This was a Zev I didn't know. It was a *me* I didn't know!

We drop into the Phonies' backyard over the side fence from Rob and Donna's.

Zev is wearing a heavy woollen hat over his hair.

We creep up to the house, to the bush underneath the living-room window where the light is on. There's a curtain which makes us feel safer. We both peep in for a flash of a second and this is what we see...

Mr Phonie's watching the TV sitting on the edge of his seat, dead serious, staring at the set as if his life depends on it. We could hear some game in progress and Zev says soccer. It's pretty intense. The crowd's going bananas, but is old Phonie yelling 'Flatten the Bombers' or whatever you yell for soccer? Nope. He's sitting there as if transfixed. The game is a close one and the crowd's screaming hoarse with excitement. I sneak another look.

Suddenly Phonie says 'GOOD!' Slaps his knees, gets up and turns off the *TV!!!!!!!!!!!!!!! IN THE MIDDLE OF THE GAME!!!!!!* The crowd is screaming and biting its fingernails to the elbow, and he *TURNS IT OFF!* We hear him moving around.

'Quick,' says Zev, 'Let's go.'

We sneak back over the fence and split.

'See you tomorrow. Talk then.'

* * *

So I'm lying straight in my long bed, in the dark night, eyes wide open. Just seeing the shadows. My arms straight beside my body, fingers straight, my long legs straight reaching down to the bottom, toes pointing straight ahead.

I'm thinking about the spying. If the police knew about it...or the parents...as they say in the cartoons 'GULP!'

Phonie...he's not interested in the game...what is so fascinating? How do you get to know what's on satellite TV? Where else do they have satellite TV? How can we watch what the Phonies are watching? I want to sleep, but I can't switch off my brain. Eventually I fall asleep hearing the crowd screaming in my head and Phonie going 'Good!'.

* * *

Zev and I sat on the school lawn and polished off lunch.

'What do you reckon?' said Zev.

'Well, he's not watching the game, that's for sure. He sees something and then he goes "Good". Something is good. Something else. The grass? The fence? The weather? Advertisements? Scoreboard? Crowd? Seagulls?...'

'I dunno.'

'We have to do more spying.'

'One thing for sure,' I said, 'we don't tell the parents.'

'Hell no,' said Zev.

* * *

I went to the library.

'Mrs White, how do you know what's on satellite TV?'

'No idea,' she said. 'Ask someone who has one...the pub on the corner.'

* * *

After school I went to the Watering Hole, pushed open the door and got hit in the face with the stink of smoke and beer.

INTERESTING FACTS ABOUT SATELLITE DISHES

1 The pub has a different sort of dish to the Phonies.

2 There is no program guide like TV Week which tells you what's on the Phonies' TV. They simply flick through the channels watching stuff from all round the world.

3 We don't know anyone else with a satellite dish.

4 They cost mega bucks.

5 Soccer might be on a UK or French channel. It could be the World Cup. Soccer's live at lots of different times depending on who's playing where.

Note: The Phonies are gone again.

20

The Blue Sky travel bag

Every now and then Stella Street has what we call a Heave Out. Everybody heaves the junk out of the garage, shed, under the house or wherever it's kept, and stacks it out in the street in front of their house. After a couple of days the council garbos pick it up and take it to the dump. In the meantime everyone prowls around and checks out what everybody else is getting rid of. If you spot something handy you help yourself.

Last Heave Out Frank scored his skateboard, and I found my bike basket and a broken golf umbrella which we fixed up and is fine. Rob always finds something to repair and sell. Donna, of course, is in heaven. If you're lucky it's like Christmas. It's amazing what people chuck out!

We were dying to see what the Phonies would heave out.

'Their furniture is at least four months old by now,' said Danielle. 'Must be time for a complete change.'

'I don't think they'll put anything out,' I said.

(Ever since Briquette's banquet the Phonies' front lawn is, for me, a historical site. Like you're standing on a peaceful hillside and your parents explain that this is the place of a historic battle and three thousand soldiers died there.)

But the Phonies did get rid of some stuff, and it turned out to be our lucky break.

The Phonies, the sneaks, waited till the last day, when everyone had gone off to work and school, and the garbos were collecting. We knew they didn't want people to go through their stuff but they didn't bank on our secret weapon —Mr Nic!

We asked him to grab anything interesting.

He said they put out a lot of empty cartons and boxes, a stool with a loose leg (practically new) which he took, and a blue travel bag (practically new) which he also took. Nothing interesting. And he saved us three beautiful boxes (all new).

'I thought you kids could make something out of them,' he said.

How could they throw out such boxes? There were two shoe boxes, one pale blue, one cream. Mrs P shops at the most exclusive shops. They were lovely strong boxes made of fine cardboard with lids that fitted perfectly. Much too good to throw out. Too good to cut up. Boxes to put treasures in. I thought of decoupaging the pale blue box like we did in art at school. Decoupage is carefully cutting out pictures and sticking them on a box so it's beautifully decorated.

The third box was a shiny black flat box, maybe for a scarf or shirt. It had sort of pearl tissue paper inside with the shop's name printed on it in gold—Chez Mireille.

The Blue Sky travel bag was ordinary and empty.

'Thanks Mr Nic,' we said, disappointed.

I suppose it was a bit unrealistic to hope they'd throw out some big clue about who they were and what they did, or new bikes or skateboards or anything we'd really like.

Zev took the blue bag, Danielle and I took the boxes and we all slouched back to Zev's for some desperately needed peanut butter sandwiches.

*   *   *

This is what happened next. Mr Nic told us later.

Not long after we'd gone there was a knock on Mr Nic's door. It's *Mrs P!!!!!* All smarmy and charmy.

Mrs P: I understand you took some items we put out for the garbage.

Mr Nic: Yes, well round here we all have a look around...see if we can find anything useful...recycling so to speak.

Mrs P: We put out garbage and we want it treated as garbage.

Then Mr Nic said she stopped for a second and changed her tune.

Mrs P: There was a blue travel bag that my husband threw out. Actually it was a favourite of mine. I would rather like it back. I wonder if you'd be so kind as to return it to me. (The very red lips smile100%, but the eyes are grey marbles.)

Mr Nic, ever kind, sympathises with her.

'Awfully sorry,' he says 'I gave it to the kids. They have more use for it, see. Always lugging things around. What about your stool? Would you like it back? I've fixed the leg. It's a lovely stool.'

'No thank you,' says Mrs P. (Red lips in a straight line.)

Mr Nic: Look, just ask the kids. They'll give it back to you. They understand about favourite things.

Mrs P: I don't suppose you'd ask them for me? (Very red lips pout a little. Charm turned on full steam.)

Mr Nic: Oh easier if you ask 'em. Just ask 'em. (The very red lips do a very thin smile.)

* * *

We were at Zev's place. Somebody knocks at the door, then Sue yells, 'Excuse me children! Zevros! Henrietta! There's someone wants to see you!'

Excuse me children! What happened to 'Hey kids!'? And as for Zevros and Henrietta!!!

We all dashed to the door to see if it was the end of the world. And blow me down there is Mrs P!

She was sickeningly friendly, and you could see she was thinking fast.

Mrs P turned it on for us just as she did at their parties. She gave us a massive smile. We could see every tooth, and the fillings up the back! Reading between the lines didn't take a crystal ball.

Mrs P: Hello children.
Hello Freak show.

Mrs P (to me): What a pretty jumper! Suits your beautiful hair! Having a good day?
Butter 'em up. Seem normal. Smarmy smarmy smarmy.

Me: Yes thank you.
None of your beeswax.

Mrs P: By mistake my very favourite blue travel bag was put out with the garbage this afternoon.
I HATE having to crawl to these twerps.

Danielle: Why did you throw it out then?

You don't have to read between the lines with Danielle.

Mrs P (giving a little laugh): Well, it was such a silly mistake. My husband, silly fellow, put it out without telling me.
Never have I met such a rude, obnoxious child.

Mrs P (voice hardening slightly): I would *so* like it back.
Give it back you little ratbags or you're dead meat.

So we turned it on for her.

Me: We'd really love to help you.
...to help you drop dead.

Zev: We'll do anything we can to help. Anything. But we put

stuff in it and took it to a friend's place. As soon as we've finished our homework we'll go round there and get it. (This was a very quick neat lie. Cool, Zev.)

Mrs P: Thank you *so* much.
I smell a rat.

Zev: When we've got it we'll drop it round to you.
When we've had a good look at it we'll drop it round.

Mrs P: Thank you so very much.
Little liar, and I don't want the little pervs snooping round our place, but what can I do?

Zev: Our pleasure!
Not!

Mrs P: See you soon.
I love you too, Spiky.

She smelled a rat.
We smelled a rat.
The whole conversation
was full of stinking rats.

Exit Mrs P.

We shot back to Zev's room. There was the Blue Sky bag. We examined it thoroughly. There's something dead important about this bag or why would she want it back so desperately?

'Hey there's a zip pocket inside!' says Frank. 'You can't see it very well because it's a little black zip.'

'Here, let's have a look,' says Zev. 'JACKPOT! There's something in it. There's a letter in it!'

Carefully Zev took the letter out like a detective (which is exactly what he was!), remembering precisely the way it was folded up in the envelope and in the pocket. We were sure the letter was important. We were so disappointed to find it was only a boring old letter to some bank.

'It must be important though,' said Zev. 'Otherwise why would she go through hell to get it?'

'We should get a copy of it,' I said. 'We'll have to give it back to her.'

We made a plan. Looking absolutely normal we all trooped out the front door. I had the bag folded flat shoved up my jumper and tucked into my jeans.

'I bet she's watching us walk up the street,' said Danielle.

We felt her eyes boring into our backs. We walked so normal and talked so normal I bet we looked really unnatural.

We walk normally to the newsagents. Zev stands guard at the door normally patting a dog that's tied up outside while Danielle normally buys candy and I make a photocopy of the letter, both sides. Carefully I put it back in the pocket just how Zev found it. The photocopy I fold carefully and put in my jeans pocket.

Then normally we walk on to Josh Laidlaw's place and normally go round the back. There's nobody home because they're at Noosa for two weeks. We wait at the back door for a couple of minutes then with the bag in hand normally walk back down the street again to the Phonies'.

Mrs Phonie has left the gate unlocked and we go up the path to the front door.

'Wonder why they didn't get a locking gate with a security phone button you press and talk?' I whisper.

'I can guess!' says Frank waving his button-pressing finger with a cheeky smile.

We're standing on the front porch having a good look around before we press the bell. In the window there's a sign saying 'THIS PLACE IS GUARDED BY A WERTMOLD SECURITY SYSTEM'. When Auntie Lillie lived here we never went to the front door. The back door was always open.

We ring the bell. Instantly there's Mrs Phonie. She must have been standing inside listening. Just as well we didn't say much. She lights up when she sees the bag, but not completely.

'Oh wonderful, you've brought it!'

She doesn't invite us inside. We aren't expecting milkshakes and chocolate cake.

Through the crack in the door we can see behind her the white hall, something that might have been a statue. Paintings. We are soaking up every detail. Eyes everywhere.

'Such a silly mistake. That man is so careless sometimes...does things without considering...'

She's babbling on at us. She's thinking about something else and we're not listening. She unzips the top of the bag ever so casually, then with the tips of her fingers unzips the inside pocket and has a sly quick little peek.

She's happy.

Bang! On goes the charm like a spotlight.

'So kind of you children to do that. This is for your trouble.'

Out of nowhere *she slips Zev $10 like a tip!*

'No trouble,' says Zev and hands the money back.

'Oh come on,' she says with a tinkling laugh. 'It's just a little reward. You'd like it wouldn't you?' And she gives it to Frank.

Once Frank's got his paws on money it stops.

'Goodbye and thank you very much,' says Mrs P, firmly shutting the door a little too fast.

You can buzz off now, I've got what I want.

End of performance.

We'd seen everything we could possibly see standing on that porch.

We went to Zaferidis' milk bar and blew Mrs P's $10 on milkshakes.

Frank and I had chocolate, Zev had strawberry and Danielle had chocmint.

Mr Zaferidis, who had just won some money on a scratch ticket, gave us big scoops of ice-cream.

Here's the letter:

First Inter-Pacific Bank
PO Box 91
Rosevale 3779

13 April

To the Manager,

I am writing to advise you that the transfer of funds you requested has been arranged as per our meeting. My wife and I are hopeful this investment will prove as fruitful as it has in your experience.

Yours sincerely,

D Hutchinson

21

The Chez Mireille box

The weekend after the Blue Sky bag business Danielle decided to do some rearranging in her room. She spread out all her cakes of soap and washcloths. Every Christmas and birthday she gets them. People must think she's a dirty person. Maybe they don't know what else to give her. She doesn't collect them but she's got an incredible collection. She has washcloths folded in the shape of a rabbit, a flower, a little duck, and soaps of all varieties and perfumes. She never uses them.

Danielle decided to arrange her soap and washcloths in the beautiful shiny black Chez Mireille box. The radio is up so loud the house is rocking on its foundations to...you guessed it...'Check out the Exit'! Suddenly the radio was turned down, then came this yell.

'Hey Henni, come and look at this!'

Underneath the tissue paper, upside down in the bottom of the box she'd found a receipt from Chez Mireille, which is a shop in Paris. Mrs Phonie had paid 750 F for something that looked like a 'chemise de nuit noir'.

'What does F stand for?' Danielle asked.

'Franc.'

'750 Franks! I didn't know you could pay for things with children!'

'That's French money, you peanut. Can I have the receipt? Next time I'm going to the library I'll look up how much it is in our money.'

One thing we know for sure—when the Phonies go away they are not just going to Adelaide.

22

Operation 'Sparks'

We showed Frank where to look over the fence to see if the Phonies' TV was on. He already knew how to ring us up.

Drrrrt drrrrt.....drrrrrt drrrrrt.....drrrrrt drrrrrt (the phone)
Frank: They're watching TV!

Me to Mum: I'm just checking with Zev on some homework. I won't be a sec.

Zev to Sue: I have to see Henni for five minutes about homework. Back soon.

Luckily it's a dark night. Like cat burglars we sneak up to the side of the Phonies' house. Zev stands right by the TV cable. Through the window we can see Mr Phonie glued to the set. It's soccer again.

'Here goes,' whispers Zev.

With the speed of lightning he whips a comb through his hair about a dozen times and touches the cable. The TV goes wild, crackling and flashing static snow.

Mr Phonie acts as if he's been electrified. He jumps out of the chair swearing like we've never heard before! Which is something!!! Mrs Phonie dashes in. He's flicking the knobs desperately trying to adjust the set. Bit by bit the flickers and flashes die and the picture returns. Mr Phonie is sweating. He mops his brow with a couple of tissues. Mrs Phonie is standing there flapping her hands. The TV returns to normal.

'If we've missed it,' says Phonie, 'there's hell to pay.'

'Oh my God,' says Mrs Phonie. 'Just what we need,' and she crosses herself.

God, this is Henni here.

You can't possibly be the Phonie's God too.
You can't possibly listen to a word they say.
It's them or me.

Henni

The game's on the TV again and they're both staring at the screen. There is a picture of the scoreboard. Suddenly Phonie goes, 'There it is! Oh you beauty! Thank God!'

He stands up, turns off the TV and collapses into his chair. 'We're not having that happen again!'

We were so busy watching Phonie putting on his performance we only just heard the squeak of the back door.

We were trapped! No time to get over the fence. A beam of light swings round the corner of the house. In a split second we dive into the rainforest. I'm half standing on Zev's foot. He's got a branch sticking into his neck.

My heart is thumping so hard I was sure it could be heard. This was Spotlight for real. We didn't dare breathe.

Mrs Phonie walks to the very spot where we'd been standing and shines the flashlight up the satellite dish cable, then she stands back against the fence and shines it on the dish. We can smell her. Then Phonie's there beside her.

'Now why would it suddenly do that? That wasn't a bird. A plane?'

'Well it wasn't bloody Superman,' says Mr P. 'An electrical

charge? Or something? I dunno.'

He grabs the flashlight and starts shining it round the place. We're terrified. He shines it down right where we'd been standing. If he sees our footprints or something in the garden dirt...suddenly Mrs Phonie gives a half-stifled scream. She's got a slug on her white velvet slippers.

'Stupid woman,' says Phonie in disgust.

They go back inside with Mrs Phonie whimpering pathetically. 'I hate all this.'

*   *   *

Next day Donna said, 'They must be having troubles with that satellite dish. There was a guy in white overalls climbing all over the Phonies' roof checking out the dish and the cable. His van blocked our drive.'

23

The fax

'Want to see something?' said Zev. ''Member Briquette's banquet?'

Who could forget it.

'Well I found this in the Phonies' garbage.' He pulled out of his pocket a crumpled piece of torn paper with writing on it.

'Oh Zev. You're not supposed to do that sort of thing. That's *private!*'

'I know.' He's still smiling. 'Have a read.'

More than ever I'm thinking 'This boy doesn't know what's right and what's wrong...and neither do I!'

It was expensive cream writing paper, and in pen someone had written names on it, branching out.

'Interesting, hey what,' said Zev. 'Know what it reminds me of? It's a sort of family tree.'

'Can you imagine the Perfumed Battleaxe and the Cowboy being interested in that sort of stuff? Do they strike you as the type to be fascinated by family history? They're not interested in old things, old folk, old anything...'

'What are they interested in? They're certainly not interested in friends. They're definitely not interested in animals.'

'They're interested in new things. Cars. Paintings. New garden. New carpet. New fence. New kitchen...new food.'

'How about money?'

Zev nodded. 'I would say definitely money.'

'I would say posatootly absolutely definitely money!'

'Sure as eggs are pineapples, money.'

'Sure as 52 is 91, money!'

'Maybe they're planning a family reunion.'

'Maybe they're figuring out who they have to knock off to get the family fortune.'

Now that was an idea!

The top of the scrap of paper was torn where the name and address had been. All that was left was the fax number.

'What about this fax number?' I said. 'How can we find out who it is? Is there a fax directory? I've never heard of such a thing.'

'Why don't we just fax them and ask them who they are?'

'What are we going to say? Who are you?'

'How about "I appear to have lost your address details. Could you please fax them to me again. Also confirm the spelling of your name. Many thanks, J. Adams"?'

I thought that was pretty neat. Obviously Zev had been working this one out for a while.

We typed it up on Zev's dad's computer and sent it off by Zev's dad's fax machine.

There were a lot of numbers in the fax number and the fax machine seemed to think about it, and clear its throat, and grumble to itself for ages before it finally said 'Transmit' and started to slowly swallow the paper.

'Well,' I said, 'it's gone somewhere!'

We mucked around waiting for the return fax.

Facsimile 852 2861 0891

'How about body faxes,' says Zev. 'You dial the numbers and feed yourself into the machine. *FeFiFoFax!* You come out a fax machine in Disneyland!'

'Or how about this, "I'm faxing you to Iceland" said the baddie, and with that his victim was faxed, never to be seen again.' Etc, etc, etc.

We waited round the fax machine for about two hours.

Nothing happened. Nothing happened. Nothing happened. More nothing. (Great stuff for an exciting plot this is!) Disappointment again. We're getting used to it. We can handle it. Disappointment is our speciality. We can take it.

* * *

'Do you want a holiday in Hong Kong?' Zev's dad says next day. 'I got a strange fax this morning. First time it's happened. You'd expect it to happen more often with the number of faxes flying round the place.'

'What was it Dad?' says Zev, so cool.

'It was a very expensive five-star hotel in Hong Kong sending someone details, prices and such.'

'Can I have a look' says Zev.

'I chucked it out. I think it's still in my garbage can. Not the sort of place we could afford.'

Zev, with a totally straight face, gave me the slowest wink in history.

24

The receipt

I was lying in bed warm and snug listening to the gentle rain falling steadily on the roof. The top part of my window framed a bit of flat grey sky. No netball this Saturday morning. The light in my bedroom was grey. It was a grey, dark Saturday morning.

Everybody was sleeping in. Danielle was reading. I could hear her occasionally turning a page. I could hear Mum and Dad talking quietly. I couldn't hear what they said, just the comfortable sound of their voices as they lazily discussed something. Sometimes they would be silent for a little while. The rain kept falling. I felt so warm and comfortable and safe.

The receipt from the Chez Mireille box was on the little table beside my bed. Mrs Phonie had bought something in that beautiful box. It cost 750 francs. She could go anywhere in the world and buy anything she wanted, but right then, snug in my own lovely bed, I wouldn't swap with her for all the candy in the world. I lay there looking at the receipt wondering what she bought and how much it cost in our money. What a strange fish she was.

750 francs. We've only got one Frank! Danielle's corny joke must have made me soft in the head. I started feeling sorry for Mrs Phonie! She was pathetic. She didn't like nice colours, she didn't like animals, she didn't like her friends. Fancy not liking your friends! Did she like Mr P? As for Mr Phonie, I couldn't even begin to think about him.

You know how you try to imagine the Queen sitting on the toilet, well, I tried to imagine the Phonies hugging each other. It wouldn't be a nice warm snuffling animal hug. It would be a spiky careful-of-my-make-up hug. And as they hugged they would be thinking about themselves.

My feeling sorry for them turned back to hating.

I decided to take the receipt to the library soon, and see what I could find out about francs, and 'chemise de nuit noir', however you say it.

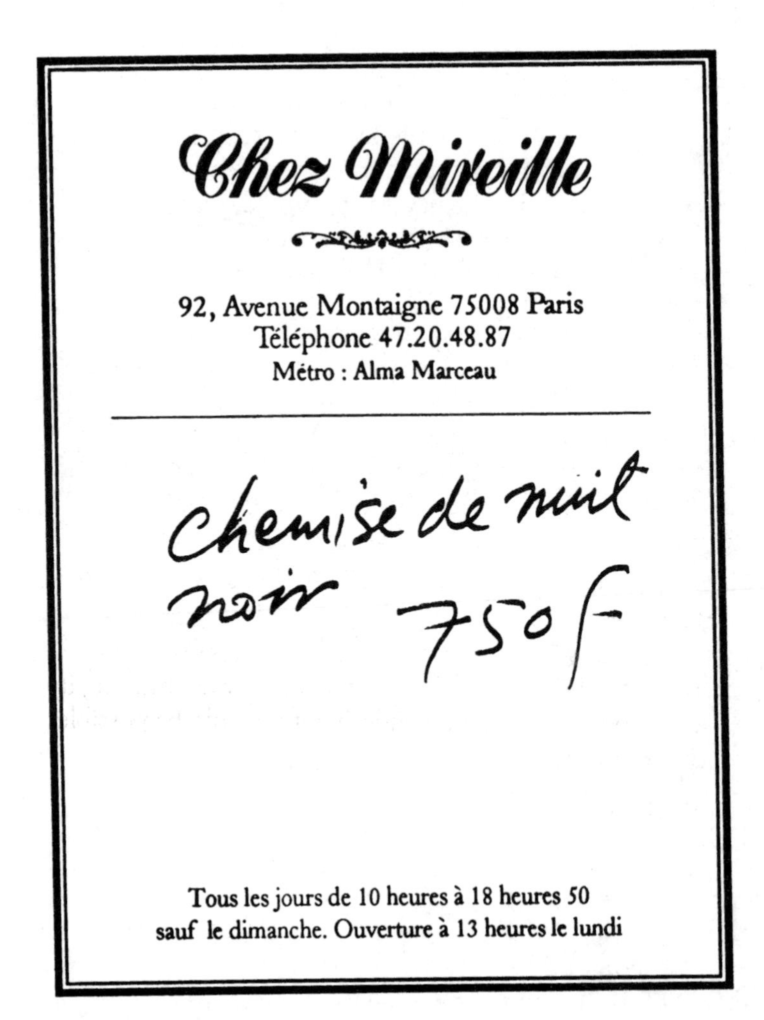

Chez Mireille

92, Avenue Montaigne 75008 Paris
Téléphone 47.20.48.87
Métro : Alma Marceau

chemise de nuit
noir 750 f

Tous les jours de 10 heures à 18 heures 50
sauf le dimanche. Ouverture à 13 heures le lundi

25

PO Box 91

It was a teachers' professional day at school. All the parents had to work. We said we'd be fine. We said we'd tidy up our rooms and work on our school projects, which sounded very suspicious, but they wanted to believe it. This was the day we'd been waiting for—our chance to visit the First Inter-Pacific Bank.

They gave us $3 each which was supposed to be for a messy meat pie for our lunch, the highlight of the day.

We pretended to be lying around, but the minute they were gone we were out of Stella Street like a flash, wearing dark glasses and hats for disguise. We spent our money on bus tickets to Rosevale, the snobby suburb where the bank was.

The bus dropped us a couple of streets away then we walked in the wrong direction, down the hill instead of up the hill, for about three streets (great detectives we are!). Then we turned the map around and walked up the hill to the post office.

We were dead lucky. Across from the post office was a cafe. We sat at a table by the window, all sharing one coke, figuring out what to do. We had a perfect view of the mailboxes. We were talking about who should have first watch, and I was thinking it might be a long boring day, and wondering if it would be possible to watch the post office and read my book at the same time.

'Hey look!' goes Frank.

All eyes to where he's pointing.

Who should be actually walking along the footpath on the other side of the street but Mrs P!!!!!!! She had sunglasses on but she was actually walking *in the street* like a *normal person!*

She doesn't walk in Stella Street. We never see them. We just see the car.

'I can smell her from here!' whispered Zev.

She walked to the post office. She stood beside the mailboxes and put her sunglasses on top of her head. Then she searched for a key and we got a glint of sun off one of her rings. She found the key, slotted it in and swung open the little door.

'Box 91!' said Zev.

'She's got a lot of letters!' whispered Danielle.

Mrs P took a large handful of mail from the box and put it in a bag she was carrying. She locked the little door, put her keys back in her handbag, whacked her sunglasses back on her nose and walked on up the street.

Zev and Danielle shot after her. They crossed through the moving traffic. Tibor would have died to see them. Mrs P walked to the end of the block stopping for a couple of seconds to look in a dress shop, then turned the corner. Zev and Danielle were not far behind.

That's all Frank and I saw. We sat and waited and waited and waited.

'No school today?' the lady in the cafe asked.

'Teachers' professional day,' I told her.

She was curious about us. I started inventing a story in my mind and was careful not to look at her. Fortunately she had quite a few customers.

Then Danielle came racing back.

'OK. Zev's waiting. Come on!' We paid quickly and dashed out leaving the cafe lady wondering.

Zev and Danielle had followed Mrs P until she went into an office building in the next street, then they waited a while just in case she came out again.

Once we turned the corner from the busy main street us four kids stuck out. A single kid on a weekday was noticeable. Four kids were unmistakable! But we all wanted to see and we couldn't think of what else to do. So in the end we all had a quick look at the building.

'What about the back?' said Frank quietly.

'Yeah! Check out the Exit!' sings Danielle. How can you be a good detective with her around!!!!!!!!!!!!!!!

We walked as quietly as we could (sounding like a team of horses) down a cobblestone alley, until we got to what we thought was the back of the building Mrs P went into. This was hard to judge because we'd forgotten to look at the number on the front. Real professionals we are!

There were bars across a large opening where people drove their cars down under. We peered through the bars. Once our eyes were accustomed to the darkness what should we see but good old $356,000! Jackpot! This is definitely where the Phonies work!

Next we decided everyone except me would wait around the corner of Acacia Drive, while I slipped into the foyer and copied down the list of businesses in the building.

140 Acacia Drive. I sneaked up the steps and pushed open the heavy glass door. My heart was pounding as I listened for the sound of footsteps on the stone stairs.

There were so many names I decided to write down just the ones on the same floor as the bank. Furiously I wrote in my little notepad, being careful to get all the spelling right.

1st floor
First InterPacific Bank
Bi-Continental Technet Enterprises
Titan Pacific Holdings
Minotaur Developments Pty Ltd
Phaedra Lynch Pty Ltd
The Kings-Stanton Charitable Trust

I hurried out the door and walked quickly away. Just as I reached the corner of Acacia Drive I glanced back, and saw $356,000 gliding off in the other direction! Just imagine if we'd been in the alley. They would have spotted us for sure. We would have been dead meat!

We caught the bus back to our place and made a huge pile of pancakes and a pathetic attempt at tidying up.

'It was a modern building, but it wasn't all that swanky,' said Danielle.

'Just because you work at a bank that doesn't mean you've got stacks of money,' I said, thinking about the bank where Mum goes. The people there don't look very rich at all.

'Should we tell the parents?' asked Frank.

'NO!' we all said in unison.

'We've got to get into 140 Acacia Drive and have a look,' said Zev.

Frank said, 'We could say we're doing a school project on money.'

'You and school projects!' we all yell.

'We may as well ask them "Are you crooks or what?",' says Danielle.

Zev was serious. 'The Phonies hate our guts. We smell a rat with them and they smell a rat with us. We can't go near the place.'

'Now think. Who could go in there for us?'

'It has to be an adult. Someone who wouldn't make them suspicious. Who could it be?'

'Well, it can't be any of our families.'

Suddenly...there are too many suddenlys in this book! I have to think of another word...Right then? Instantly? Exactly at that time? But lots of things *did* happen suddenly. Oh too bad.

Suddenly Danielle has a perfect brainwave.

'Mickie Brown!'

Remember the Brown Boys? Well they have an older brother who hasn't got a full-time job. He goes surfing a lot, and when he feels like working he just goes from door to door selling stuff, or sometimes he sells stuff at markets, like toys before Christmas. A bit suspicious. He doesn't do it all the time. He's actually quite good at it.

And the Brown Boys owed us one big favour!

26

Mickie checks them out

'Yeah...OK,' goes Mickie, 'I'll check 'em out. There's this guy I know's got office stuff. I'll sell them diaries for next year, and phone pads and stuff.'

We had it all figured out, the day and the time...and then OH BOTHER ME!!! The Phonies went away! They must have been watching the soccer again. Wouldn't it drive you mad! We put the plan on hold. This isn't one of those stories where things flow smoothly along, that's for sure.

The Phonies were away for four days. Then we got back on track.

We couldn't do it on Monday because I had netball. I forgot to say I started playing netball which is cool. I'm not very good at it. I'm not quick and my ball-handling skills are pathetic, but I'm tall which is a great advantage as you know. When the others are looking for someone to throw the ball to, there's always me standing out like a lighthouse. I'm halfway to the goal ring already.

So Tuesday was Operation Acacia Drive. Mickie was going to visit them around 2 pm, then we were going to meet him after school at the back of the box factory near the station.

Mickie was all cleaned up and business-looking, which was a bit of a shock. We're used to seeing him bashing round the place in his old jeans and surf gear.

'Well, how was it?' says Zev.

'Good!' says Mickie. 'They didn't twig to me.'

'What's it like?'

'It's just an office. Nobody works there except them. Phew, that chick wears a lot of perfume. You go in the door and up the stairs, then their door is first on the right.

'It's got all those business names on it. The window on the right when you're looking at the building from the street is their window. There's two rooms.

'She was sitting at a sort of reception desk in the first room, then another office opens off that. The door was open and Mr P was in there sitting at a desk talking on the phone to Graeme someone.

'She was pretty unwelcoming. But I showed her a lot of stuff and she warmed up. I didn't talk to him. There wasn't much around the place, like decoration or work stuff. There was one of those clocks that gave you the time in other countries and there were a couple of quality plastic potted plants.'

'That's all?'

'Yep.'

'No computers?'

'Nope.'

'A room with a big table and executives making important decisions?'

'Nope.'

'Planning white boards with a graph on it like a row of mountains going up and up?'

'Nope,' said Mickie. 'Borrrrr-rrrring.'

We all sat quietly because it wasn't how we'd imagined.

'Mickie, you're a great spy,' I said. 'That was fantastic!'

'Yeah well, I enjoyed it,' said Mickie, with a grin. 'Besides I had good sales. I sold her a couple of top-line leather-bound pocket diaries. Then I worked the building and I sold two big year planners, about six desk diaries, a couple of big diaries and a box of phone pads. Not bad for an hour's work.

'There's a couple of dentists at the end of the hall, then a cleaning company, and right next-door there's a solicitor's office.'

'Oh,' says Danielle. 'You wouldn't happen to remember the name?'

'Parry? or something?'

Guess who has the office right next-door, folks. Yep, it's Mr Slippery, our favourite solicitor in the whole universe.

'Thanks a million, Mickie,' says Zev.

'Any time,' says Mickie. 'I think it's a bit suspicious. If they are all those important sounding names they've got on the door...well, where are the people, where's all the paper, where's all the work? It doesn't add up.'

27

Birdwatching

Rob and Donna have been married for fourteen years! That's longer than I've been alive. It feels like centuries. Donna wanted to see the new Woody Allen movie and Rob wanted to go out to dinner, so they did both and we went to Frank's.

Frank was busting with news. That afternoon he'd overheard the Phonies talking and he'd heard Mr Phonie say quite clearly '...have to get Spiky, Lanky, Cranky and Twerp!'

'They're part of a gang!' said Frank. 'Real baddies! Like in the movies with scars and tattoos.'

'Eeee-vil!' said Danielle.

'Dead-ly!' said Zev.

'Now hold on,' I said. 'Sometimes I get called Lanky.'

Zev cracked up laughing.

'Hey, they're not talking about gun-infested banditos, they're talking about us! *Spiky* (he pointed to his hair), *Lanky* (me), *Cranky* (Danielle) and *Twerp* (Frank)...Spiky, Lanky, Cranky and Twerp!'

'They wouldn't be talking about us!' said Frank. 'It's their gang!'

'Want a million dollar bet?' said Zev.

It was pretty funny. The Phonies have a way with words.

Talking of words, all this time we'd been expecting another phone call from the cops, for another awful questioning about the fire.

'At first I worried about it all the time,' I said, 'but nothing's happened and now I'm forgetting about it.'

'Doesn't worry me,' said Zev. 'We're innocent.'

'Bet you're not game enough to ring up and ask the cops what happened!' said Danielle.

Zev picked up the phone. '*NOOO!!!*' we all screamed.

I said, 'Now, what do we want to do?' trying to get things back on track.

First we checked out the Phonies. Jackpot! Their TV was on soccer!

I say that because Zev and I wasted hours peering at the Phonies' TV when they were just watching it for fun. Soccer was definitely when they saw something 'good'.

I wanted to keep to the idea of spying, but we had a couple of videos to watch and the others wanted to watch them. I wanted to watch them too, but I thought we should stick to the job.

We found that by standing on Rob and Donna's bed, you could see into the Phonies' living room.

'If we could get up higher, we'd be able to see the TV,' said Zev.

'Frank, have you got any binoculars?'

'Yes, Mum's birdwatching ones.'

We got Rob's big stepladder from the shed. It was extremely tricky getting it into the house and the bedroom without knocking something flying or bashing the furniture and the walls. Zev and I carried it very slowly, while Cranky and Twerp told us what we were just about to hit.

In the bedroom we pushed Rob and Donna's bed aside and moved a chair and the dressing-table. I noticed Donna's comfy bedtime reading was 'The Abusive Relationship'. Delightful!!!

By standing with one foot on the top of the ladder, and the other on the top of the wardrobe, through the binoculars we could see the TV brilliantly. We couldn't see Mr P, but judging from the past he'd let us know pretty clearly when something 'good' happened.

Everyone had a quick look, then because I was tall and the safest on the ladder (and the most reliable, I suppose), I got the job of watching. At first I was pleased. Danielle held back the curtain with an umbrella, then they tied it with some wool.

'What if someone comes home and finds all this?' said Frank doubtfully.

'We'll burn that bridge when we come to it,' said Danielle.

'What bridge?' said Frank.

Anyway, I ended up stuck on the ladder, in a dark room, staring through the binoculars watching the Phonies' TV—boring soccer, while the others watched 'The Princess Bride', the video I picked! Being a detective is sooooooo boring!

It made me think of birdwatching. I was observing the Loaded Loathsome Abusive Twit.

Frank came in a couple of times.

'Can I have a go?'

'No, Frank. I think it's going to happen soon.'

The third time he pestered I said, 'OK, but just while I go to the toilet.'

He took over the binoculars.

'Can you see the TV?' I asked.

'Perfectly!' he said.

As I dashed through the living room the others looked up.

'Who's watching the Phonies?'

'Frank.'

Wouldn't you know it? It happened while I was in the toilet. Frank was so pleased with himself.

'It was on the scoreboard and there was something yellow, like someone waving a yellow flag. It stood out because everyone else was waving blue or red. Then Mr P turned the TV off.'

'It's a signal!' I said, 'I bet that's it! He turned it off after the scoreboard last time, and I think I saw something yellow then too!'

'What?' said Danielle.

'A signal!'

'Why?'

'Who knows? No phone calls to be traced. No letters. No way of tracking something back to the Phonies.'

We were so busy yakking on we didn't hear a car pull up.

'What on earth are you doing?' In the doorway stood Rob. He looked at the ladder, the binoculars, the curtain and us.

'Well...what are you doing?' He sounded cross.

There was a long silence, then Frank said, 'Playing fishing'.

We got the giggles. Desperately we tried to keep them in because we didn't know what Rob would do, but you know what it's like—the more you try to keep a straight face the worse it gets. I caught Danielle's eye. She looked as if she was at a funeral, but her body was shaking.

Rob grabbed his glasses off the dressing-table, then gave us another look.

'Well, put things back where you found them,' he said. We could see the corners of his mouth twitching, with a grin.

As he drove off we cracked up, cackling and shrieking. We laughed our heads off! We just couldn't stop. The words 'playing fishing' were screamingly, side-splittingly funny. Our stomachs ached. Our sides were sore. Finally the convulsions died down. But if anyone so much as whispered 'playing fishing' it set us off again.

Then we all watched 'The Princess Bride' right from the start.

28

The worst day

Some days go bad and then everything gets worse. This was such a day. I arrived home from school miserable, to find that Mum and Dad had put our couch, my favourite, the old brown couch in the Trading Post to sell it. *How could they!* When I was little and I was sick Mum tucked me up on this couch, and we've sat on it, jumped on it, made cubbies out of it, been sick on it and watched TV on it ever since we were born. This trusty, faithful, loyal, ever-comfortable old bearer *was being sold!*

A NOTE TO PARENTS

DON'T GO SELLING FAVOURITE BITS OF FURNITURE.

CHILDREN FIND IT VERY DISTRESSING!

Wait until your kids have gone to live in Russia, or Hollywood, then you can sell whatever you like. You can flog all the old stuff and swank the place up till it looks like the Phonies', but till then ***DON'T GO SELLING BITS OF FURNITURE THAT ARE PART OF THE FAMILY!***

I'm sorry about this couch outburst. I know it's not part of the story, well actually it is because it just made that day even worse. It's something I feel deeply about.

So I sat by the phone taking all the calls, telling everybody it was sold.

Voice: Can you tell me about the couch you have for...

Me: Sorry. It's ***sold!***

Voice: I'm calling about the couch...

Me: Sorry. It's ***sold!***

Voice: You advertised a couch in the...

Me: Sorry. It's ***sold!***

I think my parents got the message.

*   *   *

In my life I never think things are going to happen. I just live along. That's the way it goes.

Danielle came racing in.

'Zev's moving to New Zealand!'

No warning. Bang! Like that.

'WHAT?'

'Zev's dad's work is moving to New Zealand.'

This idea was too awful for her to be making it up. You know how they say 'My heart sank'. Mine sorted of popped. Like a balloon.

Determined not to let the tidal wave of tears that pushed at the back of my eyes flood out, I did my homework like lightning not caring if the answers were right or wrong.

I blew my nose hard and raced round to Zev's.

He was sitting on the front step with a fine black comb in his hand.

'Hi, Henni. I was just coming round to your place.'

He said it with a smile! A smile! He was cheerful!

'New Zealand?' I asked.

He nodded.

How could he be so normal about it? I could have killed him (then he wouldn't have to move to New Zealand!).

'That's putrid maggot news. Aren't you mad? Aren't you sad?'

'Nope.' Zev looked so light-hearted.

I was a whisker away from going to bed to cry for a year and he behaves like this. If he was going to play the ice game, I could play cool too.

Danielle and Frank came racing up and flopped on the lawn by the steps.

'Why are you going to New Zealand?' asked Danielle.

'Dad's computer company is opening up an office there, and they want Dad to be the boss of it.'

'What about your mum and dad and you? You don't want to go, do you?'

'Not one bit,' said Zev.

Sue opened the door, and without a word put down on the step a plate of warm-from-the-oven chocolate cake. An I'm-sorry-kids offering. (As if slices of cake could make it any better. We ate them anyway.)

'When will you go?'

'Not for six months at least,' said Zev.

'What about us, Zev? Leaving us to the Phonies. Leaving us to those wolves.'

'We'll all go and live in New Zealand,' said Danielle.

'Wish the Phonies would go to New Zealand instead of you.'

'We'll kidnap you and hide you in the attic.'

'What's an attic?' asked Frank.

'A room under the roof.'

'We haven't got an attic.'

'We'll get a hot-air balloon and all escape to a desert island.'

'We'll go to Brazil where the nuts come from, and sell doughnuts from a van.'

But all our ideas sounded dumb and pathetic because deep down we knew there was nothing we could do. This was a serious life adult decision. This was The Future and there was nothing we could do about it. We felt like powerless suffering little children.

The sun was setting. The end of this day felt like the end of everything.

'No use worrying,' said Zev. 'Six months is a million years.'

He flicked the comb through his hair and a shower of sparks shot out.

We all started laughing.

* * *

The next couple of days I began to develop eczema behind my knees and in the crook of my arms. Eczema is when your skin gets dry and red and itchy in certain spots.

The itch is unbearable. It tingles and tingles, gnawing, screaming out to be scratched. Leave it alone? Impossible. All I wanted to do was scratch the skin off my bones with fingernails six centimetres long.

I lay in bed pretending that my arms and hands were chained up and I couldn't move so I wouldn't scratch. I had this ointment that I put on twice a day and that made it feel a bit better. Going to sleep was the worst. Then I'd wake up in the morning to find I'd scratched in my sleep and there were red sores and scabs.

What could I do? Everything was going wrong. It all seemed so unfair.

Dear God,

This is the last straw. Why are you doing this to me? Is it a test or something? Is it like the plagues in Exodus, in the Bible?

You turned the river into blood. Then the frogs and the lice. Then the plague of flies. Then the disease on the cattle. Then the boils and blains upon man and beast. Then the hail and thunder and fire. Then the locusts, then last and worst you smote all the first-born children of the Egyptians.

Are these my own personal plagues?

First plague – the Phonies
Then Zev going to New Zealand.
Now eczema. Why?
What have I done?

Henni

I don't even dare to think what might come next.

29

Tears

I didn't have to wait long. Two days later I came home from netball practice and the house was strangely quiet. No radio blaring.

I came across Danielle curled up on her bed. The little tough was crying. She hardly ever cries. Not Dani.

You could chop off her hand and she'd say 'That was fun!'

When her body gets hurt that doesn't matter.

This was something deep inside.

'What is it Dani?'

She turned away hunching up her shoulders so I couldn't see her face. She was quiet. Not making a sound but sobs shaking her body.

Quietly I sat down near her. You have to watch it with Dani or you might get your head knocked off for your trouble.

'What's wrong?'

I was nearly crying just looking at her. I hadn't seen her cry for ages.

Punctuated by sobs, out it came.

'At Rob and Donna's...*sob, sob, sob*...Zev found the houses for sale bit of the newspaper...*sob, sob, sob*...and there were circles around some houses...in...(she could hardly bring herself to say the next two words)...red pen.'

Then she let go, and in a wail of tears she burst out, '*Rob and Donna are looking for somewhere else to live!*'

That does it. That's it!

My feelings for the Phonies turned into full bloom hate!

God,

I Know you say love your neighbour. But I can't love these neighbours. I am going to GET these neighbours.

I AM GOING TO GET THEM!

Quietly I said to Dani, 'No, *they* won't move. The *Phonies* will!'

Dani stopped sobbing and looked at me.

'Henni? You OK?' she said in a little voice.

'Fine,' I said. 'Never felt angrier! If you can cry I can get mad!'

30
The spider

I was watching little red spiders in a garden. They were darting about and making webs, so busy and fascinating. Then I noticed there was a much bigger spider. It was a strange one and I picked it up between my finger and thumb to have a close look at it. Suddenly its body burst open spraying my face with black poison slime. I shut my eyes tight and my nose and mouth, so the poison wouldn't get in. I screamed for help, but I couldn't open my mouth. And I couldn't see where I was going, and I couldn't breathe. I could only yell with my mouth shut, and I couldn't breathe, yelling, yelling yelling with my mouth shut, I couldn't breathe...

'Hen?'

It was Dani. I woke up just as she said it. I was gasping for air. I'd been holding my breath in my sleep.

'You were making funny noises like a strangled dog,' she said. 'You OK?'

Then Mum was standing beside her.

'You all right darling?'

'I had a nightmare.'

She sent Dani back to bed, then she sat and stroked my head the way she did when I was little, looking at me with her concerned face.

'Move over,' she said and hopped into bed beside me.

She put her arms around me. Her warm body in soft pyjamas and her smell was the most comfort I could have.

She held me safe.

I was a baby again and I slipped into sleep.

31

'The Modern Midas'

I'm hidden in the library in the grey chair, at the little red table near the corner window, hidden behind rows and rows of Statutes, whatever they are, and Acts of Parliament, which nobody ever looks at. They're probably not even books. They're probably just those boxes that look like books. Dead boring.

It's a good spot for me because I don't see anyone I know. A few times I've recognised voices of friends from school, in the kids' section of the library, laughing and talking and mucking about. Sometimes I wanted to burst round there and yell 'Listen to this!' and spill the beans. I have this secret growing in my mind. Bit by bit I'm working it out.

Remember the receipt from the Chez Mireille box? Well, I had to take some books back to the library (yes, from a school project!) and I remembered the 750 francs. How much was 750 francs? I started flipping through books on money.

These were as fascinating as a maths test, but one book, 'The Modern Midas', caught my eye. I flipped through it, and was just about to put it back when I read something that stopped me in my tracks. The hairs on my legs prickled. I burst into a cold sweat. My heart went boom, boom, boom and my brain said 'We're onto something here girl!'

Since then I have borrowed this book three times. I want to be sure I understand what I am reading. Every time I take it out for another extension of time I wait for a different librarian at the desk, otherwise I feel they might start saying things like 'Here comes the budding young criminal!' or 'Planning the perfect crime are we?'

I have an answer ready. 'I'm doing a project on Sherlock

Holmes.' So far I haven't had to use it.

This is the best place for me to read the book. I can't leave it at home. I don't want anybody to find it and start asking questions, so I keep it in my locker. After school I have a chocolate milkshake then head for the library with a bag of chips to keep my strength up.

I told everyone I'm at the library working on a project. I sure am! Biggest project I've ever had!

There was a parent-teacher interview last week. I was scared stiff Mum would say something like, 'Henni has really got stuck into that project. I've never known her to be so involved.' Mrs Finch, my teacher, wouldn't know what she was talking about because we don't have a project at the moment. Fortunately Mrs Finch is a bit slow and would have just given Mum a nice half-smile, thinking she missed something Mum said.

The library's warm and quiet, except when this smelly old guy sits near me sometimes. He has a whistle in his nose when he breathes, but he just reads the racing results and takes off.

I'm sitting here like a goldminer and I'm sure I'm digging in the right place.

32

Slam-dunk it here, slam-dunk it there

'What have you been doing?' asked Frank. 'It's like you've had chickenpox or something.'

'Yeah!' said Danielle in a put-out voice. 'Why do you love the library so much all of a sudden? What is this project?'

'OK!' I said, 'I'll tell you, but not now. Sunday morning on the basketball court. It's about the Phonies.'

'Is there a book about them?' asked Zev.

'Sort of,' I said.

'Why can't you tell us now?' said Danielle.

'Yes. Tell us now!' said Frank.

'Nope!' I said. 'We need to be where we won't be interrupted and we've got time to think.'

Then, as if she'd heard what I said, Mum yelled from the kitchen, 'Henni, help me here please.'

* * *

Sunday morning was grey with the odd splash of rain, but Mum was pleased when we announced we were going to play basketball. She was glad to get us out of the house.

'Come on. Tell us now!' said Danielle.

'Wait till we get there,' I said feeling light-headed, and excited. I felt the power of my knowledge. They were desperate to know. I was dying to tell. I ran the last hundred metres to the court with the others pounding after me.

'OK, Professor,' puffed Zev, 'spill the beans!'

'Or we'll throw you in a puddle,' said Danielle.

Zev and I sat on the back of the concrete seat overlooking the court. Briquette checked out the garbage cans. Danielle stood, and Frank sat on the basketball.

'Starting from the start,' I said. 'Remember that black box Mr Nic saved from the Phonies' garbage? Well, Danielle found a receipt in it from Paris for something which cost 750 francs. While I was in the library I went looking for how much that was in our money. There are all these books on money, economics, banks, investing, books like "How to Grow Rich", how to make money, like worm farms and stuff...what is it Frank?'

He was bouncing round like a flea.

'We should get that book "How to Grow Rich."'

'Sure. So, I was looking through this section when I found a book called "The Modern Midas".'

'What's a midas?' asked Frank.

'Remember the story about King Midas?' said Danielle. 'Everything he touched turned to gold, and then he touched his daughter.'

'So,' I continued, 'I was flipping through this Midas book, when I read about a man who bought an old mansion, ripped the guts out of it and rebuilt it. Everything was brand spanking new. Top quality.'

'The Phonies!' said Frank.

'Except it was Old Auntie Lillie's place,' said Danielle.

'So?' said Zev.

'I kept reading. Next he filled the house up with expensive

old furniture and swanko paintings.'

'The Phonies!' said Frank.

'So?' said Zev.

'And then, wait for it...he bought a mega-mega-expensive new yacht, sailed it to some islands, sold it and bought another one the same! Sound familiar?'

'No,' said Frank.

'Don't you see, the Phonies bought a new car, sold it and bought another new car. Instead of a yacht, a car! Get it?'

'Yeah...' said Zev slowly, 'but that's not so unusual. Rich people do that kind of stuff all the time. Tell us more about him. Where did he get his money?'

I paused to make it more dramatic. They were listening to every word I said. This was my big moment.

'He worked for a phoney bank!!!!!!!!!'

Dead silence.

'Cool!' said Zev.

Now to explain. I knew it would be hard, but I was the expert. I didn't read that chapter of 'The Modern Midas' four times for nothing.

'It all starts with a massive amount of money,' I said. 'We're not talking about ordinary money. This is illegal money. Like from robbing a bank, or selling drugs, or ripping off someone. They call illegal money dirty money.

'For example I'm a drug dealer and I've just done this massive deal and this is a million dollars.' I grabbed the basketball and shoved it up my jumper.

'But I can't spend this money otherwise the cops will be onto me.

'But I have some very looovely daaaaarling close phoney friends who will solve my problem.'

I tossed the basketball to Zev who was starting to get the idea.

'OK!' says Zev with a grin, and shoved the ball up his jacket. 'I'll solve the problem for you, as long as I get a slice of the action.'

'Now this kind friend,' I said waving my arm at Zev who looked pregnant, 'works for a bank. He takes the money and sends it overseas to another bank.'

Zev suddenly whipped out the ball and took a baseline swish.

'Then he sends it from that bank to another bank.' Zev threw the ball to Danielle.

'Then slam-dunks the money into another bank, tosses some of it over to this bank, slam-dunks some of it to that bank, throws it here, bounces it there, whips it out and flicks it over...slam-dunking the money all over the world.'

The basketball was being tossed around in a frenzy, bounced and flicked, and Frank was bouncing around like a ball himself. Everyone was hyper. When Zev had the ball again I yelled 'STOP!'

'OK! This clever swapping and changing and transferring is called laundering. Turns dirty money into clean money. Nobody knows where the money came from. Now my dear dear looovely friend returns it.'

Zev tossed the basketball to me.

'Now I can enjoy my money knowing that it's clean. I say I won it at the races or something and they can't prove anything! Spend, spend, spend! The Phonies are money launderers!'

Zev and Danielle got the picture, but not Frank. It's not often

Frank misses the point. 'I left my pocket money in the pocket of my shorts once and it got washed,' said Frank, trying desperately to understand.

'No,' said Danielle, 'the money isn't really dirty, it's just *called* dirty. Illegal, dirty money gets washed, swapped, changed so it's turned into legal or clean money. That right Henni?'

'Spot on.'

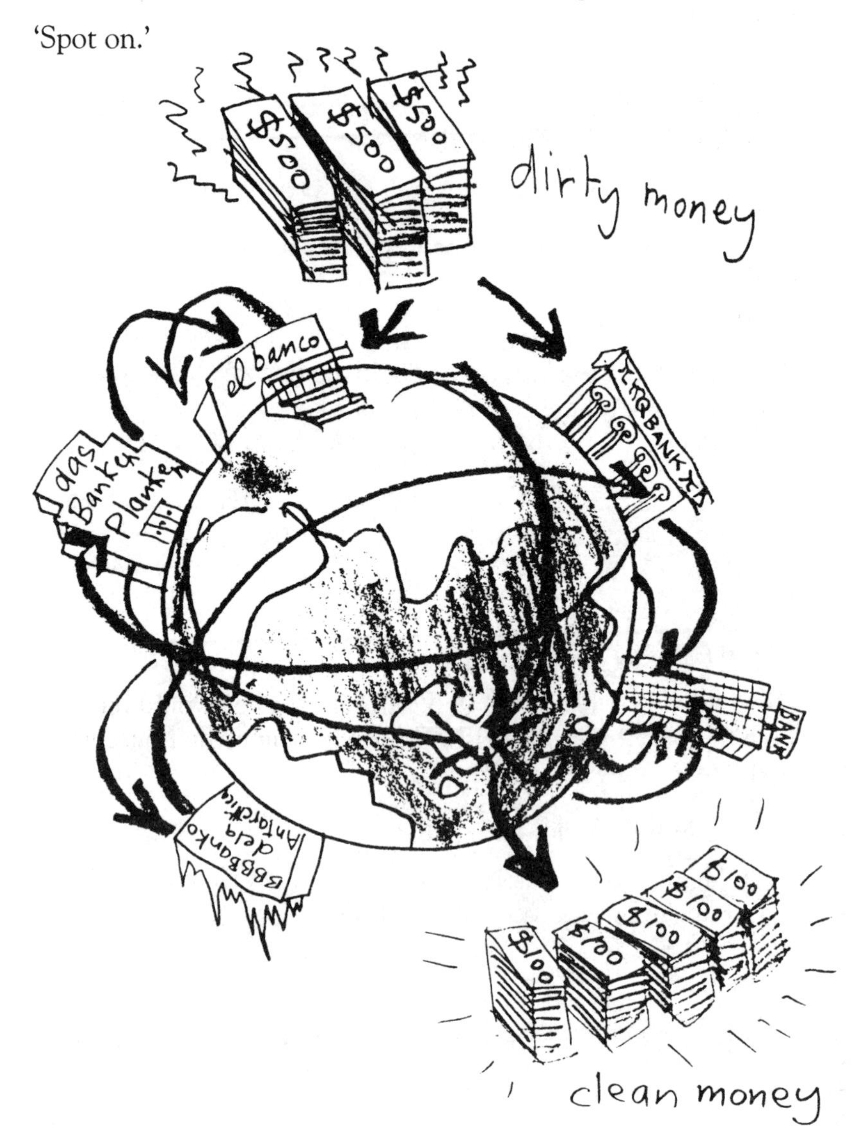

‘The new car Henni? Why would anyone do that?’ said Zev.

‘When they bought that new car, I bet the Phonies paid cash for it. The car salesman was probably so pleased to sell such an expensive car he turned a blind eye to all that cash. Then they sold that car for nearly as much as they paid for it, and bought another one, so the money’s been sort of changed three times.’

‘I bet they pay cash for everything,’ I said. ‘The trick is to change the money. Say you’ve got six hundred $50 notes, you swap it for three hundred $100 notes, or...’

‘A million Mars Bars,’ said Frank.

‘You’ve got it Frank!’

That kid’s amazing sometimes.

‘Swap the Mars Bars for a holiday in Disneyland. Nobody’s going to know where the money came from!’

‘OK,’ said Zev. ‘What’s the deal on the paintings?’

‘Well, they probably bought them at an auction, and paid cash for them, and when the time is right, they’ll sell them again. Presto! Clean money!’

‘What about the house?’

‘I bet they paid all the builders with cash. They would have bought everything with cash. Probably bought the house with cash.’

‘Why are they always travelling overseas?’

‘I’m not sure, but I bet it’s something to do with moving money round the world.’

‘Smuggling?’

‘Could be.’

'What about the First Inter-Pacific Bank?'

'It's probably just a name. A shed on some little Pacific island.'

'And those other names...Bi-Continental Thingo Whatsit...'

'Names.'

'What for?'

'To fool people.'

'What do you think?' I asked. The others were revved up, but I had the feeling Zev wasn't 100 per cent convinced.

'We haven't got proof,' he said slowly.

'What about that letter in the pocket of the Blue Sky bag. Transfer of funds. Remember?'

'I think I believe it,' said Danielle. 'I'm sure they're dishonest.'

'I want to believe it,' said Frank.

We talked about it all the way back from the courts and were so deep in conversation we walked right past our gates and got to the end of the street before we realised.

Here's what we decided:

* Zev will read 'The Modern Midas', especially Chapter 9.

* We haven't got any real proof so we won't tell anyone.

* We will continue spying, especially trying to find out what Mr P sees in the soccer games on TV.

* It seems like it could be true.

While I was doing the drying up that night I kept thinking about money.

At home nobody ever talks about money. Mum and Dad never talk about it. It's just there in Mum's purse or Dad's wallet. I don't know how much money Mum makes, or Dad.

Mr Nic's on the pension but I don't know how much that is.

On Fridays we get our pocket-money.

We're not rich but we're not poor.

Sometimes when I want something trashy Mum says 'No!'

'Why can't I have it?'

'Because it's junk and we can't afford it.'

But if I'm desperate for something like a new Gillian Rubinstein book, if I plead for it enough (usually three or four days) and set the table without being asked and generally crawl for it and be nice to Danielle—eventually, we *can* afford it.

On holidays money seems easier and Mum and Dad are more inclined to say yes than no.

*　*　*

Later on as it was getting dark I lugged the garbage can out onto the street. Lovely old Stella Street looked so quiet and friendly. I thought I must be nuts to think this is all going on in 45. In the book they were talking about hundreds of thousands of dollars, even millions. I must be going off my rocker! Like Frank said, it was just something we wanted to believe.

I looked at the old house. Then I had a strong sad memory. I saw Old Auntie Lillie's frail white fingers dipping into her purse to give us each a coin, and her sweet smile.

Then Briquette barked. There was a note of alarm in her bark. My anger came back. Yes, it *could* be true.

This next bit seems like one of those amazing coincidences you only read about in books, but I swear it happened.

That night I was sitting on the old brown couch watching the news with Dad.

On came an item about some fraud court case where some business man has ripped off the savings of thousands of people.

'Blood-sucking reptile,' said Dad shaking his head in a world-weary way. 'Honestly! It makes me spit nails, those smart operators. Think of all those poor people who worked and saved and trusted their money to this get-rich-quick ratbag. Imagine, all those years of hard work and saving, then suddenly, WHIP! The money's gone! Honestly, it'd break your heart.'

Then we saw the baddie coming down some steps with the police. He had his coat over his head so you couldn't see his face.

'Well, they caught him,' said Dad, 'but I bet there's a whole stack of others who just slipped through the net.'

He gave me a kiss with his scratchy chin. 'Well, Henni my dear, the only way anyone in this family is going to make any money is by good old-fashioned hard work. And for that you need good old-fashioned sleep. Time for bed, Henni my dear. Goodnight sweetheart,' and he gave me another scratchy kiss.

33

Bertie the Second, and the parcel

Another hard thing to do in this writing business, is to leave out all the bits that don't really belong to the story. For example, about this time, I came second in a state-wide fiction writing competition, but it's not part of the story so I won't mention it, or the fact that the judge said my entry 'showed great promise, the style fresh and the story compelling'.

He he he he he he he! (That's me chuckling in a self-satisfied way like Mr Bean.)

Another thing that happened was Heap, real name Marcus. He was a rent-a-kid that Donna, Rob and Frank had for two hard weeks. He could have a story all to himself. Every bit you could see of him was pierced. He did one thing. He made us all feel lucky, despite the Phonies, and 'The Future', compared to him.

And I won't tell you about Rob going to an auction and buying an old 8 mm projector with a stack of films which we played forwards and backwards a million times, especially the film on swimming and diving and the man eating spaghetti. We had to go to the doctor to get something for our laugh muscles.

And I won't tell you how we found a mobile phone and thought it was the answer to our prayers until we found it wouldn't work.

But I will tell you about Bertie because he certainly played a part in the story.

Zev and I were on our first daylight mission to the Phonies' because we noticed the garage door had been left slightly open.

We thought the Phonies were away but we weren't positive, particularly as they'd left the door open. Besides trespassing, we knew it was dead dangerous so we were going fast, sticking to the bushes at the edge of the garden. Suddenly...

'Ullo! What ya doin'?' came this scratchy voice.

'Nothing!' We both froze with terror.

'We're sunk!' I whispered to Zev.

But nobody came forward. Who was it? We looked around feverishly but couldn't see a soul.

'Ullo. What ya doin'?' the crabby old voice said again.

'Nothing, honestly, well...something, but nothing bad or anything...' We searched for the person we were talking to.

Then Zev gave a funny laugh-squeak.

'Look! It's a cockie!' he whispered. He pointed out a bedraggled bunch of feathers with its head on one side eyeing us suspiciously from the apricot tree.

'Ullo! What ya doin'?' he said again.

Silently we cracked up, mighty relieved. We abandoned our mission, made the fence in two strides and dropped back over into Rob and Donna's. We advanced slowly on the apricot tree. The cockie was still sitting there, his black beady eye watching us.

'Ullo! What ya doin?'

'We're catching you,' said Zev.

The cockie stepped from one foot to the other as we approached and bobbed up and down in a little dance.

Zev walked slowly up to the lower branch holding out a thick stick. The cockie stepped right onto it as if he had been waiting at the bus stop and the bus had just arrived.

'Ullo! What ya doin'?'

'We're finding you a home.'

We took him to Mr Nic.

'Ullo! What ya doin'?' he said to Mr Nic who was bent over the radishes in his garden.

'Thinning out my radishes,' said Mr Nic without thinking. Then he turned round to see who had spoken.

'Ye Gods and little fishes,' said Mr Nic standing up with a wobble. 'What have you got there?'

He peered at the bird as if he was seeing someone he hadn't seen for fifty years.

In reply the cockie put his crest up and did his little jig.

Immediately Mr Nic put out his finger and gave him a little tickle behind the ear, if he had an ear.

When he was a boy Mr Nic had a cockie called Bertie. First off he imagined he was seeing Bertie again.

Needless to say he took to the cockie and was delighted to have him, but insisted we put up COCKIE FOUND signs around the area.

He called him Bertie the Second.

But to get back to the story, as Mr Nic collected his gardening things he closed up his shears, pinching his hand.

'Blast!' (This is as strong as Mr Nic's language gets.) It obviously hurt.

'Now that reminds me!' said Mr Nic forgetting his hand in a second and turning to us with his shaggy eyebrows raised and his watery eyes blinking quickly.

'There's something I've been meaning to tell you!'

Every day since the Bully Burgess dog catcher nightmare Mr Nic has been taking Briquette up to his place. This day, just as he's collecting Briquette from 47, a courier van pulls up outside 45. The driver opens the back door and goes to take out a fair-sized heavy box. The door swings back and whacks him on the hand. He swears.

'You OK?' goes Mr Nic.

'Yeah,' says the driver rubbing his hurting knuckles. Then he goes to the gate of 45 with the parcel, but of course the gate is locked.

'How am I supposed to deliver something if I can't get in the gate?' says the driver, angry.

Mr Nic says, 'Beats me. Look, I live up the street. Do you want to leave it with me and I'll drop it round when I see them?'

'Thanks, but no thanks,' says the courier. 'I've got to do the right thing.'

He puts the parcel in the back of the van, and gets on the radio to HQ. (HQ—Headquarters—Mr Nic uses a lot of old army expressions.)

HQ says the driver's a bit early. The parcel wasn't supposed to be delivered until after 10 am.

'And I got a good start today too...it's just not my lucky day.'

So he sits in his van for a while and he and Mr Nic talk about dogs. He's a border collie man. Mr Nic says he's just dog-sitting but he's more a terrier man. I can just imagine them babbling on. What great company dogs are...how intelligent...how faithful...bla, bla, bla.

Still nobody shows up from 45.

In frustration the courier gives a mighty ten-second blast on the horn. Mr Phonie shoots out the front door towards them.

'Bit hard to deliver things when you can't get in the gate,' says the courier.

'I thought it was open,' says Mr P, no apology or anything.

He stares daggers at Mr Nic as if to say, 'What the hell are you doing here?'

Briquette starts barking at him. Mr P signs the courier's form and takes the parcel inside.

The driver starts up the van.

'And I've got a pick-up here on Friday the thirteenth!' he says to Mr Nic as he drives off. 'Think I'll wear a suit of armour for that one!'

'What was the box like?' we asked.

'Cardboard taped up with brown packing tape. It said SPORTS-RELATED EQUIPMENT on the side.'

He did us a drawing of the box with rough dimensions marked on it. It was a good drawing. When Mr Nic worked at the railways he had a fair bit to do with parcels.

'Bit peculiar,' said Mr Nic. He sort of dislocated his top false teeth and ran his tongue around the top of them. 'They don't seem the sporty type to me...'

34

The longest day

This is the longest day of my life. This will go for pages. That's another thing I haven't figured out—how writers get all the chapters about the same length.

I find some bits of the story are quick and belong by themselves and others are long. This bit sure is long. You know the title Stella Street and Everything That Happened? Well this part is where a lot of everything that happened happened. So fasten your seat belts, and if you're reading this under the blankets, make sure there's plenty of life in the flashlight batteries.

You couldn't half tell it was the big day. The night before, Frank laid his action clothes out on the floor, ready for the morning. They looked like somebody already. Donna told us this later.

I was twittery and jittery. Scared. Thought I'd never get to sleep, afraid I wouldn't wake up. If I thought of what might happen I felt faint. Drop clear to the ground and wake when it's all over. I felt very responsible for Danielle and Frank. We had argued and argued. Zev and I said they must go to school as usual. And they said they *had* to come too. Hadn't they been involved *all along*? If they were left out they would *never never never never never never* be our friends again.

In the movies at this point they always say 'How did we ever get into this mess?'

I was scared one of our parents would twig that something was up. We pretended it was a normal Friday. Fortunately we had been rehearsing for a special assembly at school which we'd talked about a lot. As we walked out Mum said, 'Good luck with the rehearsal.' Phew! Thank goodness!

Everybody left for work and school as usual. We walked a couple of blocks then doubled back to Frank's via the back lanes. Frank had left the back gate open. We sat whispering and waiting in Rob and Donna's garage with 'our' parcel.

This was an old grey-green metal box. During the war, it was packed with eight shells to fire at the enemy, except now it was packed with four old pineapples from behind the supermarket and last year's phone books. It was neatly sealed up with brown packing tape in a cardboard box that said FRAGILE—SPORTS-RELATED EQUIPMENT.

We heard Mr Nic's old Mazda pull up, then Zev and I carried our box out. Quickly we put it in the trunk, all piled in the car and drove off. We had to fit around Mr Nic's long parcel.

Mickie Brown was waiting for us by a phone booth in High Street. Mickie was fantastic. He looked absolutely believable. He had on a sort of smart track-suit top over a white sports shirt with navy slacks and shiny black shoes. It crossed my mind that Mickie could be in films. He always played the part so well.

We sat in the car outside the JetExpress Cargo Depot chewing minties provided by Mr Nic. Sure enough, at five past eleven a van pulled up. The driver carried a very heavy carton into the depot, then left.

'That's the guy!' said Mr Nic.

Considering we'd never actually seen the Phonies' carton ours was a pretty good copy. The cardboard on ours was a bit darker.

Go!

Mr Nic walked into the depot up to the express counter with his long parcel.

'Now young man,' he said to the guy, 'this is very precious. It contains half a dozen spears. My son was up in New Guinea in the '50s and was in a bit of a skirmish and...'

Mickie strode in carrying our box and put it down right beside the Phonies' box and started filling in the label identically.

'...collector's items. I believe one of these spears actually killed a man. Perhaps I should insure them...'

We were lucky. The JetExpress depot, a big barn of a place was fairly busy. A couple of chaps were packing bags in a van. A forklift truck was buzzing around. The guy at the express counter had a cold. His eyes were streaming. Every couple of minutes he fished a large crumpled hanky out of his pocket and blew his clogged up nose.

Mickie had to wait while the guy showed someone how to complete the form.

'Collecting one, dropping one off,' said Mickie so convincingly.

'I am in rather a hurry,' said Mr Nic.

Cold-in-the-nose shoved a clipboard at Mickie and turned to Mr Nic.

'...I wouldn't have a ghost of an idea what six spears'd be worth to insure...'

Although us kids were sitting quietly in the car, we felt as jumpy as grasshoppers in a jar.

Mickie picked up the carton and walked out of the depot. He put the carton in the trunk of the Mazda, gave us the thumbs up sign and walked off. That was the plan. It was as easy as that.

Then a minute later Mr Nic came back to the car chuckling. 'I've just insured four lengths of dowel and sent them to my brother in Bundaberg.'

'We've done it, we've done it!' we yelled.

But as we pulled away from the curb, a black BMW that we hadn't noticed, on the other side of the road, did a U-turn and came after us.

Suddenly it was scary again!

Mr Nic drove straight to the cop shop. This was our plan. The cops would open it properly in front of everyone. Simple. No hanky panky. And we wouldn't get blamed for stuff we didn't do. We were sure what would be inside.

The cop shop wasn't far. Mr Nic knew the names of all the streets by heart. The car followed us and parked up the street.

Quickly we lugged the carton in, dumped it on the counter of the police station and told the cop on duty that we wanted to see the most important person in the police station. Detective Sergeant Thomas and another young guy with his hands on his hips (plus all the police hardware), were curious to know what these kids and this old man were on about.

We insisted they open the parcel.

'What is it? What's inside it?'

'We don't exactly know but we are absolutely sure it is *very* suspicious and we know the people who sent it and they are *extremely* suspicious people.'

'Is it a bomb? Where did you get it? What evidence do you

have? Do you realise you may be up for stealing?'

We badgered them furiously.

'If you don't open it now you are blowing a once-in-a-lifetime opportunity.'

'If we're wrong what harm is done?'

'We'll tape it up. We'll deliver it back to the depot. We'll apologise.'

'Promise!'

'Except we're *positive* we're not wrong.'

The young cop cut the tape on the parcel with a Stanley knife. He folded back the flaps. There was a styrofoam box inside. In came a man in a suit. It was the guy who followed us from the JetExpress depot.

'Let me introduce myself. Bryce Perry. I'm a solicitor and I believe this carton belongs to my clients.'

It was Slippery! What an evil looking weasel! He was so full of himself in his snazzy suit. There were daggers coming out of his eyes at us. He was thinking 'Thank God. I made it in the nick of time'.

'What do you think you kids are doing?' he said ignoring Mr Nic. 'If the parcel is returned now we won't press charges.'

'Keep opening! Keep opening!' we yelled at the cop with the Stanley knife in his hand.

'Yes, open it up,' said Slippery, his voice so cool and smug. 'Let them make total fools of themselves.'

Whatever it was that prompted him, pure curiosity, heat of the moment, wanting to settle it once and for all, maybe the daggers coming from Slippery's eyes, the cop cut the tape on the styrofoam box and lifted the lid. Inside there was a strong leather case, like one for a musical instrument, closed with a couple of clips.

The cop lifts the case out and flicks up the clips. He opens the lid and there are two flawless shiny black ten-pin bowling balls nestled in protective sponge.

I was the only one who said anything. We were horrified.

'Oh no!' I gasped.

Slippery is smug, but furious. His eyes are slits as he looks those daggers at us.

'Just what are you kids up to? You're causing a lot of trouble. What did you think you were going to prove? These are two competition-class bowling balls supposed to be heading for the world championships in Rome and my client is not going to be happy if they don't arrive in time. There will be hell to pay. I hold you personally responsible. Your parents are certainly going to know about this. You should be at school, you inconsiderate bumptious sly little no-goods.'

He totally ignored Mr Nic, which was incredibly rude.

He turned to the young cop. 'What kind of parents have these brats? Dregs! Criminals! They just let them run wild!' He moved towards the case.

Then everything happened.

Zev grabs a ball and runs. The cop nearest to him goes to stop him, but Frank sticks out his foot. He trips and crashes to the floor. People underestimate little Frank. Zev is weaving through the building. Those balls are heavy enough to hold, let alone run with.

I don't know how, but he makes it out the back door, to the yard behind the cop shop. He dashes to the fire escape stairs, with everybody racing after him. The cop's shouting, 'Stop you idiot. What do you think you're doing?'

Nobody knows what's happening or where he's going. He's up the fire escape stairs at the back of the building—clatter clatter clatter on the metal stairs. Screaming voices echo in the canyon of buildings.

I'm climbing too. There's another cop close behind me—clatter clatter clatter—who's trying to grab me by the shoulder, but netball is paying off. My ball-handling skills are not great but my ducking and weaving is hot. I dare not look down through the metal steps or I'll be sick. I have no idea about Danielle and Frank. But there's so much screaming and shouting behind me I figure they're following somehow.

As Zev passes a second floor back door he sets off an alarm. We zig-zag across the back of the building, getting higher and higher on the metal stairs. It's so noisy. I hear myself gasping for breath and the blood pulse in my ears. I dare not look up to see where Zev is. I'm watching every step.

The alarm is wailing and wailing. Everything's out of control. I hear Zev furiously clattering on. The cop behind him is hot on his heels. He practically has him.

Zev reaches the top, a split second before the cop grabs him. With a last mighty heave, just as the cop yells, 'GOT YOU!', Zev hurls the ball four storeys to the ground.

We hold our breath. The ball falls past us in slow motion, then with a deafening crack, the black ball hits the concrete. It explodes into a million pieces, releasing what looks like a huge flock of papery birds that flutter up towards the sky. Money!

In that split second of silence, when we had our eyes out on stalks and our mouths wide open, Danielle shouts with joy, 'That's not a bowling ball! That's a Kinder Surprise!'

* * *

Slippery, who had Danielle in a half-nelson, dropped her arm and changed his tune completely. Goodness gracious me! What has happened? Can I believe my eyes? Has somebody done something naughty? A pathetic change of tune. Kids at school could kill him any day.

Of course the cops want to know everything. Where were the bowling balls from? Where were they were going? And a couple of cops are given the job of picking up the money, and Mr Nic insisted on being a witness. Slippery says, 'My clients left for overseas yesterday.'

Frank whispers to me, 'What's "my clients"?'

'The Phonies.'

'They did not!' he whispers. 'I saw them last night at 45.'

The police held us for further questioning. Questions, questions, questions. Police spend all their time asking questions! We desperately wanted to get back to Stella Street to check out 45. It dragged on and on. Felt like hours and hours. Later we found out it was really only an hour.

The cops were frustrated and short tempered because they were so busy. There had also been a robbery in the shopping centre. They didn't really want four kids making a mess of their cafe-bar leaving clouds of hot chocolate dust all round the place. Frank found some bubblegum in his pocket, and kept popping it till he was driving us mad too! We sat and waited and waited and waited on seats in the corridor and went to the toilet at every opportunity.

They weren't having any luck contacting our parents either. Eventually they were so fed up, they took our names, addresses and phone numbers and said they would call us later in the day for questioning. Mr Nic was still helping with the money.

We took off.

35

The chase

We belted back to Stella Street. It took us an hour by bus and running, till we got the stitch. Zev and I left the others. We crept up to 45 as if it was a bomb about to explode. Total silence. No movement. No sign of life. We slipped round the side of the house to the window and peeped in. Everything was in its place, neat and clean as if the residents had stepped out for a moment.

'Dam busters!' whispered Zev. 'They've shot through!'

'Gone? Without taking any of their stuff?'

'Would you hang round to pack? I bet Slippery tipped them off by phone.'

Then he clenched his fists and hammered them.

'Double dam busters.'

I was shocked by the fierceness of Zev's anger. I stood there asking dumb questions. 'Where to?'

Suddenly he was moving.

'Grab Frank and Danielle. Grab money. Meet you outside 47 in two minutes. *RUN!*'

He raced back to his place.

I dashed home.

Danielle was feverishly cutting a huge sandwich.

'Danielle! The Phonies have gone. Come on! Come *ON!* We've got to meet Zev. Get your money box.'

'What?'

'COME ON! Grab your money box. *Quick!*' Just as we raced out with Frank, a taxi rounded the corner. There was Zev racing towards us.

'Get in!' he yelled.

'Where to, guys?' The driver was surprised at this hyper-frenzied load of kids.

'The airport! Fast! Quick! Urgent!'

'Stella Street's all flying off today, are they?' said the driver.

'What do you mean?' I asked.

'There was another cab called for Stella Street to the airport, about five minutes ago,' he said, 'I just missed it.'

'I *knew* it,' said Zev punching the air.

We felt the thrill. The mad roller-coaster was taking off again.

'You kids got any money to pay for this?' asked the driver.

Danielle rattled her piggy bank.

The taxi driver started getting into the mood of it, he took a turn sharply.

'How much to the airport?' said Zev.

''Bout 25 dollars.'

'No worries!' said Danielle handing her half-eaten sandwich back to me.

She brought down her shoe heel on the piggy bank with a mighty whack.

It smashed to smithereens in her skirt. (It was a day of explosions!)

'Yikes,' said the driver but kept driving.

Danielle sat in the front seat of the taxi, with a pool of broken piggy bank and her savings in her lap. As the meter ticked over she counted the money into her shoe.

'*Must* be urgent!' said the driver.

'We're meeting some very close friends,' said Zev.

Zev dropped his voice. 'This is what we do when we get to the airport. Our friends will be there somewhere. You're supposed to check in your luggage and get your seat a fair while before the plane leaves.'

'What do we do when we find them?' asked Frank.

'We'll think of something,' I said.

'First we find them,' said Zev.

'How?'

'International terminal?' asked the driver.

'YES!' Zev and I said loudly at the same time.

'How do we do it, Henni?' asked Zev.

'Stick in pairs,' I said. 'And we need a central place to be home base and we report back there every three minutes.'

We twisted and turned through suburban streets with enough stop lights to make your hair frizzle, then suddenly we slipped onto the freeway and we were flying.

'Danielle, you go with me. Frank, you go with Zev.'

The taxi charged up the ramp and screeched to a halt outside the international terminal. Danielle emptied her shoe into the driver's cupped hands.

'There,' she said, 'that's exact.'

She pocketed the rest and shook the broken bank from her skirt into a garbage can as we raced into the terminal.

'There's home base!' I yell, pointing to a big cut-out kangaroo in the centre of the terminal.

'Meet at the 'roo every three minutes,' says Zev. 'You this end, us that end. They're *here* somewhere. Go!'

The terminal is packed with people. A whole flock of jumbos must have just landed. People moving in slow chattering herds, the loud buzz of excited talk, groups of friends, families, tearful grandmas, hugging and meeting and luggage everywhere. We squeeze around people, bursting through queues, tripping over bags.

''Scuse me...'Scuse me.' We thread our way. A couple of times I think I see Mr P but it's just a look-alike.

At first I try to spy like they do in the movies, hiding behind things and sneaking looks, but it's impossible. There are just too many people. Air New Zealand has a massive rugby team all loud and strong and laughing. I accidentally trip a huge burly rugby player.

'Watch it kiddo,' he growls.

Skipping and stepping over cases and through people, eyes everywhere, heads whipping round we search for the Phonies' faces.

We race back to the kangaroo just as Zev and Frank puff up.

'No luck so far.'

'It's so *crowded!* We could easily miss them.'

Qantas flight 20 for Hong Kong now boarding from Gate 9, last call for Qantas flight 20 now boarding from Gate 9.

Every departure announced over the loudspeakers sends the dread of failure through us.

'See you in three!'

People carry stacks of duty free stuff and kids clutch drinks, kids clutch teddies, kids clutch parents. A little kid in new basketball gear sits on top of a huge pile of luggage on a trolley. Serious businessmen in serious suits stride round the place with briefcases. A rowdy group of Japanese make an obstacle race out of their huge golf bags.

'Henni!' says Danielle. 'I'm busting. Phonies or no Phonies I've got to go to the toilet.'

'Oh, *great* Danielle! Just what we need.'

'Wait for me here,' she says and dashes off. I am furious. Every second precious and I'm waiting for her to go to the toilet! I wince at the sound of a plane taking off. She takes forever. Meanwhile I am looking my eyes out.

Suddenly Danielle's back, all arms and legs waving like one of those hanging toys with a string you pull to make them dance.

'I've smelt her! She's there. It's *her!* For sure! In the cubicle next to me! *I'm positive!*'

Should we report back? We might lose her.

'You stay close to her Dani. I'll report back.'

I race back to the 'roo. Hell. I'm too late. The boys aren't there.

I dash back from the 'roo to the washrooms and enter expecting to run slap bang into Mrs P. Danielle's reading the notice on the tampon machine as if it's the most fascinating thing she's ever read.

'She's still there,' she whispers.

We wait around the corner at the wash basins where we can see the toilet doors in the mirror. It's pretty crowded. A door opens and out comes this woman with thick curly brown hair, in a smart greenish tracksuit, big dark glasses and a yellow shoulder bag. She is flustered and doesn't even stop to wash her hands. As she walks past us we bow over the basins. And there is that absolutely unmistakable smell—*MRS PHONIE!*

'Disguise!' I whisper, 'Hang on a sec...'Scuse me.'

I dive into the cubicle ahead of the queue. Stuffed down behind that garbage can thing there's a Georges bag with a light pearl-coloured plastic coat and a purple scarf. It's Mrs P all right!

Air New Zealand Flight 25 for Hong Kong now boarding from gate 12. Last call for Air New Zealand Flight 25 now boarding from gate12.

The people in line look cross as I shoot out the door.

No Danielle. She's followed Mrs P.

Now I'm looking for Mrs Phonie *and* Danielle. My heart is pounding and my hair prickles. We've found her! Now what do we do?

More grandparents say goodbyes to more grandchildren. Businessmen read papers. I nearly go head over heels over a pair of skis.

'Don't run please,' an airport official barks at me. 'Slow down, young lady, or you're heading for trouble. I've been watching you kids.'

I see a flash of green tracksuit through a mob of people near the newsstand.

Qantas Flight 43 now boarding from gate 3. Last call for Qantas Flight 43 now boarding from gate 3.

I look at my watch. Back to the 'roo.

'*We've found her*', I gasp out. '*Positive!* Danielle's after her, but I've lost her and Danielle. She's wearing a brown wig, a green tracksuit, big sunglasses and a yellow bag.'

'Yessssss!' says Zev with a hiss like a snake.

'No sign of Mr P.'

'If she's in disguise he's going to be too. Great! And we look just like us,' Zev says. 'Give us your hat Frank!'

He covers up that hair.

'Mr P will have to change in the men's washroom.'

'Check 'em out.'

'We need home base down that end,' I say. 'The newsstand. There's a big display of Paul Jennings books near the postcards. Meet you at Paul Jennings in three!'

I find Danielle studying the leaves of a big potted plant outside the Golden Wings Lounge. I am so relieved.

'She's in there! She went in there! She's in there!' she says pointing to the Golden Wings Lounge. 'Mr P's probably in there too. They're in there.'

'Stop saying they're in there! Is there another door out of this place?'

'Check out the Exit!' she squeaks with one of her crazy rolling eyeball looks. 'Don't know. We can't go in there. They'd chuck us out.'

A waiter strides towards the lounge.

''Scuse me,' I say. 'My aunt is in there. We're waiting for her. Is there another door out of here in case we miss her?'

'Yes,' says the waiter, 'there's a door round the corner near the bar. Would you like me to tell her you're here?'

'Um, no thanks! We want it to be a surprise!'

He gives us a conspiratorial wink and swings through the door.

A friendly looking blonde lady bounces towards the lounge. Danielle pounces.

'Our auntie's in there and we're waiting to surprise her. Could you do us a favour and see if our uncle's in there too? She's wearing a green tracksuit and she has curly brown hair and big sunglasses.'

'Hang on a sec,' says the blonde lady disappearing inside. In a moment she's back.

'No, your uncle hasn't turned up yet, and your auntie is looking a bit worried. But I won't say a word.' She smiles and goes back in.

Alitalia Flight 86 now boarding from gate 6. Last call for Alitalia Flight 86 gate 6.

'Hey!' squeaks Danielle, 'from by this pillar I can see people coming and going from both doors!' She stands guard.

I race back to Paul Jennings.

'She's in the VIP lounge. And he's not. Any luck with him?'

'Nope, but I've thought of something. You know those family names on the hotel paper from Briquette's banquet?'

My mind's too busy. This is no time to stand round sprouting bits of sudden inspiration!

'Tell me later.'

Zev's pleased with himself. 'Give me that stuff. I'm nearly as tall as her aren't I!'

I can't believe it. He ducks behind a pillar and puts on Mrs P's coat and scarf shoving his jacket in the Georges bag.

He wends his way through the crowd. Suddenly he feels a

mighty shove in the back.

'For God's sake woman get changed!' this voice hisses. 'Meet me in the wings.'

Zev lopes off to the Ladies, sort of trailing the Georges bag so Phonie won't see his hiking boots. I don't see Zev get the shove in the back, all I see is Zev (Mrs P) going into the Ladies! So, with my head down, I hide in some large Greek ladies and scuttle in too. There's Zev (Mrs P) standing in the line.

'He's going to meet her in the wings. What's the wings?'

'The Golden Wings Lounge. She's there now.'

'Sure?'

'Yep, Danielle's watching.'

Singapore Airlines Flight 16 now boarding from gate 5. Last call for Singapore Airlines Flight 16, now boarding from gate 5.

Out we go, Zev stripping off as we run.

We see Frank first in the distance, then Danielle beside the pillar waving furiously. There's Mrs P all right accompanied by a guy with a beard! Instant beard—nice one Mr P! They both see us. That instant we all start running. We're all strung out chasing the Phonies.

'I've had enough,' says the airport guard stepping in front of the Phonies with us close behind. 'I don't know what you're up to but you're all coming with me.'

'No we're not!' says Mr P and socks the guard in the jaw out cold.

'Yes we are!' says Danielle in a white rage and sinks a kick into his shin that would have scored a goal at fifty metres.

'YOU **@#$!#$&✠v#F¬x*@%* KIDS!!!!!' yells Mr P.

Another guard gives chase. He's way behind. The Phonies twist and turn. We're all spread out. I bump into an old man. Danielle knocks cans flying off the trolley of the man refilling the coke machine. The Phonies double back and make a dash for the automatic doors to the departure lounge. The doors start to open. There's Zev by the side wall, with his hand on a fuse box. Furiously he's flicking *three* combs through his hair! The doors stop. The gap is too narrow for a person to fit through.

The Phonies swing round and dash to the escalator. They bound up it. Somehow Danielle's beaten them. With a whoop, and a nifty little skip she sinks the toe of her old shoe into the emergency stopping button.

The escalator jerks to a halt. The Phonies practically fall, see her at the top like a bad dream, decide they're closer to down than up, and belt back down the escalator towards me! I'm racing towards them, but what am I going to do? Close behind me the guard yells 'Stop where you are!'

Where's Frank? I look round for him.

The guard grabs Mr P who turns around and slings him a punch on the side of the head. I heard the awful thud of it. I feel sick. And scared. At the start, it felt like a thrilling game but not any more!

The Phonies run right around a pile of luggage and straight into a blind corner. There's no escape. There's an elevator but it's on an upper floor. Desperately Mr P presses the button. Danielle is nearly at him. Another guard is shouting to people to get out of the way.

Where's Frank? I can't see him anywhere. I've lost Frank.

Mrs P is whimpering beside the pile of luggage.

Suddenly Mr Phonie grabs Danielle and holds a gun to her head!!!!!!!

God! God! God! Not Dani!
Please! Oh please God, Not Dani!
Give me all the other plagues,
the lot, but not Dani! Please.

He has one arm around her neck, the other hand holds the gun to her head. Danielle is frozen, but on her face which is squashed sideways, not fear, but an expression of blazing anger.

Please God! Don't let Dani do
anything stupid. Send a miracle...
Just a little miracle. Now!
Please!

The action stops dead. Nothing moves except the light above the elevator. The elevator is coming down. Only one floor to go.

Then a little hand shoots out from the zip of a surfboard cover. I'd know that skinny wrist anywhere.

The little hand slips bubblegum just under Phonie's foot.

Phonie, half-dragging Danielle, takes a heavy step back. He looks down at his foot to see what he's stepped in.

Danielle belts the gun out of his hand. It spins across the floor. Quick as lightning she pounces on it. When Danielle is excited stand back. Take cover. We're all scared. She fumbles with the gun as if she doesn't know if she's left-handed or right-handed with it, and crouches like they do in the westerns, sort of pointing it at the Phonies.

Mrs P faints clean away.

Mr P does a double-take. Then he looks down at his wife and screams, '*BLOODY* **#%@%$# ^ %$#$* *IDIOT!*' When the chips are down, she's on her own. He looks like a dangerous cornered dog, his eyes wide and one corner of his neat beard has come unstuck which makes him look even more off his head.

The airport guard has an I-can't-handle-this-mess look on his face. Danielle gives a pleading look to Zev and in that split second Mr P takes off. Boy can he run! He's going like a cut cat!

'*Leave him Zev!*' I scream. '*It's too dangerous!*'

I could still hear the thud of the punch, but Zev's after him.

Mr P, going like a bat out of hell through the crowd, dives around a corner and vaults onto a moving walkway. He gets up tremendous speed.

Zev races beside the walkway. Mr P twists round to see who's after him. That second, Zev, whipping the combs through his hair, springs down and slaps his hand on a panel in the side of the walkway.

Zev's hair stops it. Mr P, travelling at a great clip, hurtles headlong down the walkway into a family. The mother with a toddler in her arms is knocked back onto her husband who slams back onto the stroller with the baby in it. Unbearable, heart-rending screams go up. They must all be seriously injured.

Mr P jumps away, and sprints downstairs to the automatic opening doors that lead to the outside parking lot.

Zev won't give up. He tries to stop the doors but picks the wrong control box and sets off a hideous alarm. Mr P bursts out of the building. He weaves through the parked cars thinking at last he's lost Zev, anyway that kid couldn't do anything weird out here.

On the driver's side of $356,000, Phonie, gasping for breath, fumbles for his keys. The time he takes to find them is just long enough for Zev, keeping low, to make it to the passenger side of the car. Phonie stands pressing the remote-control central locking button on his keyring. He presses and presses. Why won't it work?

Out of sight, Zev crouches by the car, eyes shut, furiously flicking the combs through his hair.

Phonie tries and tries and tries to get the alarm thing to clear. He wrenches at the locked door handle. In an explosion of temper he hurls the keys at the car and kicks the driver's side door.

'YOU **%&#¬b^2✘✠$#$@*&$##!** OF A THING!'

Zev, slumped against the car, exhausted, sees Phonie running slowly from the airport parking lot, towards the highway. Then out of the blue, the retreating figure of Mr P is brought to the ground by a truly awesome flying rugby tackle.

It's Rob!

* * *

What a mess! The family on the walkway were rushed to Emergency. Planes were delayed. People swirled around. No one quite knew what was going on. An announcement was made that there had been a slight disturbance and everything was now back to normal.

Rob, still getting his breath back, and two airport guards brought Mr P inside, handcuffs on his wrists and a guard with his arm through each arm.

'ROB!' We were ecstatic! 'How come you're here?'

'Frank rang me.'

Frank had a smile as big as the sun. 'Stella Street: TWO. Phonies: NIL.'

Mrs P was just coming round, the centre of a massive ring of onlookers. Danielle marched up to her and with one quick flick plucked off the wig.

'You *little bitch!*' screamed Mrs P at this final indignity.

'Lovely to see you again,' said Danielle.

'Always felt we neighbours should get to know each other better,' said Rob. 'What line of business are you in?'

The Phonies ignored him.

'They're the First Inter-Pacific Bank,' said Zev.

'And Minotaur Developments,' said Frank.

'And Bi-Continental Technet,' I added.

'And Kings Something-or-other Charitable Trust,' Danielle chipped in.

As we said this Mr P looked like concrete setting.

By then there were 53 airport guards and six thousand policemen. Where were they when we wanted them?

'I've given you such loyalty,' whimpered Mrs P, as she and Mr P were led away.

'What do you want?' snapped Mr P. 'A receipt?'

36

After the airport

On the way home Frank and Danielle were high as kites but Zev and I were quiet.

'The family on the walkway?' I asked.

'Yeah,' said Zev, 'I can't stop thinking about them.'

'Me too.'

We told Rob.

'No use stewing. Ring up and find out.'

He pulled in beside a phone booth. It took a couple of calls to get the answers. The nurse said the little girl had a broken arm, and they were very bruised, but amazingly that was all. They had just come back from a lovely holiday. She told Zev to stop worrying as there was nothing he could do about it. Maybe he could visit them tomorrow to apologise and explain.

'Happier now?' asked Rob.

'Much!' said Zev.

Like the sun dawning on the first day of summer holidays, it was dawning on us that we had probably got rid of the Phonies.

In books they say, 'She felt a sudden surge of happiness...' Well, I did!

'I can't *believe* what happened!' said Danielle.

'Frank, how did you ring up Rob?' asked Zev.

'Got the money from Danielle. I stood on phone books and a

New Zealand lady helped me. I didn't have the right coins. She only had New Zealand ones, but they worked.'

'Thank goodness!' said Rob.

'Zev, what were you going to tell me, you know, when we found Mrs P and I said tell me later?'

'Oh yes,' said Zev, pleased. 'You know that piece of hotel paper with the family names on it, from Briquette's banquet? Well, when I heard she was in disguise, it came to me. You know when you pretend to be someone else, you have a new name, new family and everything, so if the cops ask who you are, you have your story ready. She was learning a new family, I bet you a million bucks that's it.'

'Danielle,' said Frank slowly, 'what did it feel like when he had the gun...you know?'

'Some of my hair was caught on his shirt button, and it was really hurting. I was so angry. The gun was like a hard thing against my head. I didn't think about it. It didn't seem real.'

She pressed her thumb hard against Frank's head. 'It felt like that.'

'Hey Danielle, I wonder if you'll get a $500 fine for stopping the escalators,' I said.

Rob had been listening and laughing.

'This calls for a celebration! It's Friday night. No school tomorrow! Let's have a word to the others.'

I got a real shock when I walked into my bedroom and saw things as I'd left them that morning. It was still the same day! It seemed like six months later.

We had showers, got changed, and went to Zev's. We ordered fish and chips from Jaws, the expensive fish and chip shop that delivers (their chips are divine, and they make their own fabulous steamed Chinese dumplings). The champagne corks popped.

'To life without the Phonies!' said Rob.

'TO LIFE WITHOUT THE PHONIES!' We raised the roof!!

'Let's hope we've smelt the last of her,' said Frank.

Then, in a higgledy piggledy fashion, with interruptings, rememberings, dead accurate sound effects, impersonations and slight exaggeration we told our extraordinary story to the disbelieving parents.

'Life's going to be a bit dull after this,' said Dad.

Donna glanced at Rob. 'Don't bank on it,' she said, and flaked out in a chair.

'I can handle it,' said Rob giving her a grin.

Poor Mr Nic looked dead beat, but like all of us he didn't want to miss anything.

'Mr Nic, what was it like picking up the money?' asked Sue.

'All that dough!' he said wistfully. 'We had a laugh, I tell you, those two police officers and me. We kept each other honest. It was all hundred dollar notes. My goodness it must have been packed tight. We picked them up and picked them up until they might just as well have been autumn leaves.' He held up his knobby hands. 'This afternoon these hands held well nigh on $400,000 cash. I'm stiff from picking up money!'

'How was it when Mrs P fainted!' said Danielle.

'Wasn't that awesomely cool! She went like this,' said Frank and buckled at the knees.

'She just sort of went plop,' goes Danielle, then for ten minutes we're all fainting like Mrs P.

'Attention! Attention! I have some news,' said Tibor.

He sat in the big lounge chair with such a cheeky smile he looked like a court jester, with the audience waiting for his next trick.

'Well then tell us, for God's sake,' said Dad.

'Or we'll faint like Mrs P,' said Donna.

'Don't start that again!' said Mum.

Tibor stood up and cleared his throat. 'You may have wondered why it is we had such quality champagne on hand this evening.'

'I did wonder that!' laughed Mum.

'Here's the reason. It's 99 per cent sure that we're not going to New Zealand. I'm leaving the company and a friend and I are going to start our own little computer business here.'

Our whoops and yells set all the dogs in the neighbourhood barking. Briquette went crazy. She thought it was all for her. If humans get emotional, dogs get over, over emotional!

'We've talked about it for ages,' said Sue beaming. 'It seems like now's the time.'

'So, my friends,' said Tibor, 'you'll have to put up with us for a bit longer!'

Dear God,

Just look at us. Have a look in my heart.
Words seem so silly.
Thank you. Henni

Zev didn't know whether to laugh or cry. He gave Tibor and Sue such a huge long hug I'm sure he was hiding the tears. Danielle was dancing. She was as hyper as Briquette. Frank sat on Rob's lap, smiling.

As for me, in my mind I had a black dark corner, a part I called 'the bad room'. I used to shove the rotten piece of information in the room and slam the door. I suppose I shut my mind off and refused to think about it. Well, someone had just flung open the door.

'Now you'll need a good name,' said Rob. 'How about Comput-Tech-Serve-Net Bi-Pacific Holdings International?'

'And a good solicitor,' said Dad. 'We know one who's just lost his main client.'

Sue laughed the happiest laugh. 'Yes, we thought if it doesn't work we'll set up as private detectives. Tibor will process the info and the kids can do the legwork.'

'How much did you know of what was going on?' we asked.

'We guessed some,' said Mum. 'We knew you were watching them.'

'Playing fishing! That was a real beauty!' said Rob.

'We talked about stopping you,' said Mum, 'but we knew that would be like a red flag to a bull. So we did...'

'Nothing!' said Rob.

'Although, if I knew then what I know now...' she trailed off, wrapping her arms around Danielle.

Briquette was asleep on my feet. Frank was asleep on the floor. Mr Nic was asleep on the couch.

* * *

This story does not have a neat ending. You know, like those mysteries where everything is explained, for example, that was why that happened, and this caused this. Our story isn't one of those jigsaw puzzles where all the pieces finally fall into place. So it's no use looking down the back of the couch, or going through the contents of the vacuum cleaner. The pieces don't exist. The picture will never be whole.

For example, nobody ever found out who tried to burn down the Phonies. The red comb was a red herring, so the cops plagued us about the fire, when it was probably someone criminal and dangerous who did it. The Phonies weren't at all helpful to the police. Wonder why not?

After that Friday, 45 was crawling with cops, and of course we had to go to the police station and answer endless, endless questions.

The cops mentioned a couple of times a strange 'power surge' that blew some electrical stuff at the airport, but they didn't ask us about it, so we didn't tell them.

Our big question was 'Where did the money come from?' Was it all rip-off investments? Mr Nic is invited to a barbecue at the house of one of the cops he picked up the money with. He's going to ask about it.

We never found out about the Phonies' parties, but they were pretending to be a normal business, so we think it was probably some of their investment 'clients'—suckers!!! One thing is for sure, no friends called around to water the garden and pick up the mail. One day a moving van showed up and carted all their stuff away.

The soccer games on TV? We think we got most of that one right. Mr P was watching for a signal, from near the scoreboard. The police thought it might have been his brother, in France. Next day they'd be gone, maybe smuggling money from somewhere to somewhere. And Zev was right about the paper with the names on it being a new family for the Phonies.

Another thing. In stories, they put your photo on the front page of the paper saying what heroes you are. This did not happen. There was no reporting of it at all because the cops were onto something big and kept the lid on it, while they continued investigations. We had to keep quiet.

Detective Sergeant Dave Watson (the one who questioned us about the fire) said the police recognised our intelligent hard work and the risks we'd taken, however, in future we should leave it up to the police. He shook our hands and said when we were older we should consider a career in the force.

'It's all over,' said Danielle.

'But what about the big reward?' said Frank. 'In stories they always get lots of money for a reward, and a medal. There's always speeches and a reward!'

37

Spring

It was spring. At the milk bar Mr Zaferidis had stuck up on his shop window the word SPRING in flowers cut out of magazines. It looked like something a Grade 3 kid had done, but we understood the feeling.

Our lilac was flowering, and across the front of our verandah the wisteria was dripping flowers.

It was spring and Donna's garden was in full bloom. All the little plants just bust their buds for her. They flower like crazy. It is something to see.

We were lying in her garden.

Two girls were looking over the fence at Donna's garden which is not unusual because lots of people stop to admire it.

'Great garden,' said the oldest girl who had a round freckly happy kind of face.

'Yeah,' said Frank. 'My Mum grew it.'

'It's fantastic,' said the other girl with straight hair, their eyes taking it all in.

Briquette was looping around chasing a butterfly as if her life depended on it.

'Is that your dog?' said the smaller girl.

'Yeah,' said Frank.

'What's her name?'

'Briquette.'

That set freckles and straight hair both off laughing but not in a mean way. And we were smiling at them laughing. Then they disappeared. They were nice. They must be visiting someone in the street we thought.

Suddenly they were back, this time at the gate, the eldest girl carrying a big cardboard box.

'Can we come in?'

We looked at each other.

'Sure,' said Frank.

'These are for your mum,' the girl said offering the box. 'Our mum's a potter. Here's a box of her flops. Your mum can plant flowers in them.'

Inside the box were the most fantastic wobbly wonderful crazy pots with cracks and chips and colours to knock your eyes out.

'Where do you live?' says Frank.

'45,' the two sisters said at the same time.

'Jinx!'

THE END

I could say the next bit or I could finish it now. You'll just think I made it up so the story has the happiest ending any story could have, so I wasn't going to put it in.

PS But I will because I can't keep the secret any longer.

Donna's pregnant.

Isn't that fabulous!

For our friends living beneath
the Pelaco sign, with love.

Designed and typeset by Elizabeth Honey

First published 1995 by Allen & Unwin Pty Ltd., 9 Atchison Street,
St Leonards, NSW 2065 Australia

Thanks to Kate Repka for her assistance.

Annick Press Ltd.

Cataloguing in Publication Data

Honey, Elizabeth
Stella Street, and everything that happened

ISBN 1-55037-515-6 (bound) ISBN 1-55037-514-8 (pbk.)

I. Title.

PZ7.H76St 1998 j823 C97-932648-6

Distributed in Canada by:
Firefly Books Ltd.
3680 Victoria Park Avenue
Willowdale, ON
M2H 3K1

Published in the U.S.A. by Annick Press (U.S.) Ltd.
Distributed in the U.S.A. by:
Firefly Books (U.S.) Inc.
P.O. Box 1338
Ellicott Station
Buffalo, NY 14205

Printed and bound in Canada by Webcom Limited.